FAITH

ALSO PUBLISHED BY DAWN PUBLISHING

The Relentless Rebel Duology by Dawn Bates:

Friday Bridge – Becoming a Muslim; becoming everyone's business (1st Edition, 2013; 2nd Edition, 2017; 3rd Edition, 2023)

Walaahi – A Firsthand Account of Living Through The Egyptian Uprising And Why I Walked Away From Islaam (1st Edition, 2017; 2nd Edition 2023)

The Sacral Series by Dawn Bates:

Moana – One Woman's Journey Back to Self (2020)

Leila – A Life Renewed One Canvas at a Time (2020)

Pandora – Melting the Ice One Dive at a Time (2021)

Alpha – Saving Humanity One Vagina at a Time (2021)

Anthologies:

Break Down to Wake Up – Journey Beyond the Now by Jocelyn Bellows (2020)

Standing in Strength – Inspirational Stories of Power Unleashed by Laarni Mulvey (2021)

The Potent Power of Menopause – A Culturally Diverse Perspective of Feminine Transformation by Dawn Bates and Clarissa Kristjansson (2022)

Alive to Thrive – Life After Attempting Suicide: Our Stories by Dawn Bates and Debbie Debonaire (2022)

Memoirs/Biographies:

Crossing The Line – A Journey of Purpose and Self-Belief by
Dawn Bates (2017)

Becoming Annie – The Biography of a Curious Woman by
Dawn Bates (2020)

Becoming the Champion – V1 Awareness by Korey Carpenter
(2020)

Unlocked – Discovering Your Hidden Keys by Carmelle
Crinnion (2020)

The Recipe – A US Marine's Mindset to Success by Jake Cosme
(2021)

Self-Help:

51 Powerful Ps of Public Speaking by Krystylle L Richardson
(2022)

ManUp: Tough to Talk: Reducing Male Suicide and Destroying
the Stigma One Story at a Time by Steve Whittle (2024)

Fiction:

The Democ-Chu Series by Nath Brye:

Slave Boy (2020)

Blood Child (2021)

Sin Eater – Memories Vanish When She Appears by Amanda
Denham (2024)

To discover the latest Dawn Publishing books, please visit
https://dawnbates.com/readers

FAITH

LEAVING RELIGION TO SAVE YOUR SOUL

DAWN BATES

DAWN PUBLISHING

Published by Dawn Publishing
www.dawnbates.com
The moral right of the author has been asserted.

For quantity sales or media enquiries, please contact the publisher at the website address above.

Cataloguing-in-Publication entry is available from the British Library.
ISBN: 978-1-913973-41-4 (paperback)
978-1-913973-42-1 (ebook)

Book cover design – Jerry Lampson
Publishing Consultant – Linda Diggle

To discover more about Dawn Bates, her travels around the world as she continues to write her own books, whilst supporting other authors, make sure you sign up for her regular emails using https://dawnbates.com/dive-in

Are you a writer? Do you want to get published? Then make sure you visit the home of Dawn Publishing at https://dawnbates.com/writers and see how Dawn can help you on your journey to becoming published!

Dedicated to

K.O.M.A and N.O.M.A.

As well as all those brave enough to question everything,
seeking their own truth and then stepping into living it.

"It is not your faith that makes you kind, it is your heart
and your morals.
It is not how you dress that makes you pious, it's your
actions and your words.
It is not your study of books that makes you wise, it is what
and how you learn with and from others, and then how
you implement that knowledge to make the world a better
place."

Dawn Bates

CONTENTS

PREFACE

Within the various religions around the world children are being abused, families are being destroyed and communities left poor to fund temples, synagogues, churches, and mosques.

Over the centuries we have seen religion destroy countries and masses of people slaughtered, and those 'at the top' do nothing to protect 'their flock', and in many cases are deeply involved in the abuse themselves, or at least part of the cover up.

Abuse against women and children is widespread across all religions. Whether it is the Catholic priests and nuns with their vows of celibacy contributing to the sexual and ethnic abuse of children across the world – especially in the North American Indian Schools, rape and sexual abuse by Rabbi's or Jewish teachers in school – with the family of the victims being ostracised by the rest of the local Jewish community, or the sexual and mental abuse by Imam's within the Islamic faith.

No religion is innocent of these crimes, nor are they

innocent in covering up or excusing the devastating crimes the religious leaders commit against the most vulnerable in our society.

But it is not just sexual abuse, there is also financial abuse where money is donated to the synagogue, the church, the temple, and the mosque in order to 'honour the almighty' even if it means that your family starves in the process. We see this financial abuse from the streets of New York to the slums of Pakistan and on the banks of the river Amazon. Nowhere is safe from the financial corruption of religion.

Spiritual and emotional abuse is also widespread within the religious communities and takes many forms, including competitiveness in who is the humblest, the most devout, most pious, and most active in spreading the word of the holy book of choice. Religion used to give people the feeling of belonging, a sense of refuge and safety, but with the number of sexual abuse cases coming to light over the last fifty years, terrorist activities from fundamentalists in *all* religions, and the awakening of many who are on a deeper journey of questioning, many more people are leaving organised religion.

For centuries we have seen Christian missionaries travelling to far flung places of the planet and spreading the word of Jesus and discrediting the spiritual beliefs, natural healing remedies and connection to the earth of the indigenous communities, thus indoctrinating tribes and communities into believing in one form or another of Christianity, removing them from their ancestors and traditional practices – and ultimately losing connection to who they are on a deep soul level. The conversion of

Africans to Christianity and then shipping them to the United States of America during the decades of slave trading has meant many of the black communities within the United States of America now celebrate the very thing that tore them away from their heritage and ancestral home.

On a more localised level, we see members of the congregation, qahal or ummah – all words which represent the term community – shaming one another for not being pious, generous, humble, or zealous enough, with members of the religion passing judgement on one another which goes against the very teachings of all Abrahamic faiths, as the only one who can pass judgement on any of us is the Almighty. For a member of any religion to pass judgement on another in terms of their spiritual practices places them on the same level of the Divine Almighty, the gravest sin of all.

Land used to build places of worship shows the religious leaders have lost the understanding of just how beautiful our planet is, and that to be in nature is a gift, a trust from God, Allah, Universe, Source, Dieu, G-D, The Creator – whatever name you wish to give to what I now call GUS – God Universe Source. People are forced, by shame and guilt, to worship inside a building instead of worship the land and the wildlife that inhabit it, placing manmade sculptures above natural beauty and design.

As for Faith's story, it may be written from an Islaamic point of view as we met through Islamic circles, coming together in a deep bond of friendship when we both observed the daily lives and practices of others, regardless of religion – be it Judaism, Christianity, Buddhism,

Catholicism, Hinduism et al – so many who could recite scripture from perfect memorisation, living their lives being holier than thou by attending their chosen place of worship, donating money and their time to charity, and yet were so quick to judge those who appeared to have less than them, could not quote scripture off the cuff and did not have a place to live.

We saw and experienced ostracisation of those who splintered themselves away from the mainstream religious groups, and saw homelessness, poverty and hunger ignored, when the places of worship could have easily opened their doors to those seeking shelter, food, and support.

Faith and I understood that so many who follow religion, follow blindly, choosing to focus solely on studying a single scripture without studying and comparing their chosen holy book with other scriptures, with even fewer studying history, sociology, cultures, psychology, and politics which would give an even greater depth to their belief and understanding of our humanity.

The teaching of religion, from those whose belief is based solely on scripture, without the expanded knowledge base of these additional subjects, in our opinion provided a weak foundation – and it was this shared understanding that brought us together, deepening a friendship which was too short, a friendship which was never really given a chance to flourish over a lifetime – but in the time we knew each other we both flourished, deepening our faith, even if it meant that we both 'strayed from the path' more and more towards Sufism, mysticism and the quantum realm.

Faith's story is an example of what happens on an

almost daily basis for those of us who see how abuse is hidden in plain sight, and how for those of us who choose to step out of the religious communities to put faith into action are persecuted and banished from our communities and families.

It is an example of how even in the toughest times when we have to stand alone and pursue our own path away from everyone and everything we know, it is the deep faith we have in ourselves, in the Divine, and the 'greater plan which we are destined to live out' which keeps us grateful and moving forward in times of difficulties.

Faith in action is what Faith lived by on a day-to-day basis, taking what he learnt in the pages of the Qur'aan, the holy texts of Judaism, Christianity (in all the different guises), Buddhism, Taoism, Sikhism, Hinduism, Mysticism and Shamanism along with the endless stream of books which were with him everywhere he went. Everything he read, he questioned, internalised, and then he carefully chose the aspects he would put into practice from what he knew.

His way of life was unsettling for many and confronted those who believed themselves to be more righteous and devout, more knowing, and more religiously evolved. His purity of faith was beautiful, inspiring, and humbling, and as you will read in these pages, the less religious he became, the deeper his faith grew and the more he created dangerous enemies who claimed to live a holy life.

I know his story will resonate with many, and I am glad we used to joke together about telling his story, because now I get to share it with you all in the hope that you too will stand true in your faith, in who you are and what you believe.

There are many lessons in this story for all of us if we choose to be open to them.

And in the words of Morcheeba, one of our favourite bands, *Enjoy the ride!*

ONE
STONED

"What do you mean he is dead? When? How?" Another friend dead, a friend who was younger than me, took his health and well-being seriously because for him it was one of the greatest gifts Allah had ever given him.

Such a sweet, kind, and generous soul, one who took the gentle practice of his faith seriously by putting into action everything he carefully contemplated after reading more books than anyone else I had ever met.

"He was stoned," came the reply.

"Stoned? He overdosed on weed?" came my reply.

"Trust you to think of that kind of stoned. I mean he was stoned to death, in a town square in Pakistan."

Confusion, an inability to comprehend the words I was hearing and put them together to understand what my friend Samira was telling me. Tears burning the back of my eyes, and a deep sadness overwhelmed me, not unlike the sadness I had felt upon hearing the news that my beloved friend Amira had died just a few months earlier.

The disbelief turned to disorientation, sending a wave

of nausea over me. It was intoxicating, all-consuming and no matter how much I tried not to imagine what had happened, my mind was trying to put together images of what I imagined it would have looked like. How could I believe the words I had just heard? I looked at the boys sitting on the rug in front of me, and not wanting them to be in ear shot of the conversation, I grabbed my coffee and headed to my bedroom.

I hadn't even gotten up from the couch before the tears had started falling. How could this be? Amira and now Faith? Death happening all around me in Cairo due to the bloody uprising and a husband so caught up in the reporting of the political events with the BBC, along with the Start Up Cairo events, he was never home for me to cry on his shoulder and be held by.

Closing the door behind me, I lay on the bed hugging the pillow tightly, swallowing the sadness and the pain, whilst also silently screaming the pain into the pillow.

"Moana are you still there?" asked Samira. "I am so sorry to tell you this news. I know you and he had a close bond, the pair of you 'rebels' together."

"I just don't understand, I mean I do… understand what you are telling me, but why? Where in Pakistan? Who did this? Who did he go with? What was he doing out there?"

"Moana slow down! You'll choke yourself on your own questions!" said Samira snapping me out of my cascade of questions, whilst so many more were flooding my mind.

"Yeah, sorry, I just can't…" I stammered and cried whilst trying my best to breathe. I went quiet so Samira could fill me in on the details, the tears fell one after the other, my mind swimming with confusion and rage at those who had killed my friend.

"We are still finding out what happened exactly, but it was in a village between Multan and Karachi – which could be anywhere given the distance between those two places. All we know is that when he arrived in Multan, he was heading to Karachi to get a plane back here. He had a few more places he was going to visit, such as Rahim Yar Khan because he wanted to visit Patan Minara the 5000-year-old Buddhist Monastery – and you of all people know how he loved history and the evolution of religion. We know he was then going to Khairpur to visit and draw some of the historical monuments, as well as get some of the silks and leather for his mum and dad. Where he was going between those two we have no idea. We don't even know if he had made it to Rahim yar Khan."

"So how do you know he was stoned then? If you don't know where it happened and where he was, how do you know it was him? There has to be some kind of mistake. This is Faith we are talking about. He wouldn't even wave his hand at a fly to get it off his dinner for heaven's sake!" I cried into the phone.

"I know he wouldn't. And we know it is him because the local news reports in the Hyderabad press showed a picture of him with the title 'Pakistani man killed', not 'British man stoned', just that he was Pakistani and had been killed. They also found his documents, but it isn't making international news yet, not that any of us have seen anyway. His cousin in Kashmir told the family that Faith was protecting a lot of the women he met, educating them, and teaching them about the choices they had in life and helping them escape abusive marriages with a few underground organisations he'd hooked up with; so, we think he was either killed protecting someone else, or he'd been targeted for the work he was doing. As it is being reported in Hyderabad rather than Multan we are assuming that he had already been to Rahim Yar Khan and left. You know there will be an international cover up Moana – or it will be linked to some kind of bullshit story about him being an infidel corrupting the minds of the local people." Samira's voice broke away and I could hear her sobbing gently on the other end of the phone. We cried together for what must have been ten minutes, without words, because there were no words. There was just pain, sadness, and disbelief that our dear friend had been killed in such a terrible and painful way.

"Hey habibiti," was all I could say as my own tears continued to fall. We cried together, thousands of miles apart, mourning the death of our friend; a friend who was one of the most interesting, funniest people we had met. A radical in the most beautiful of ways when it came to religion, faith, love, and community. Now he was no longer with us, having been killed by one of the most violent and evil displays of human behaviour possible, and by those who prayed to Allah five times a day.

To know that he had suffered in such a way, to have stones thrown at his body, breaking him in the most unimaginable ways, physically, mentally, and emotionally. I then let out a small laugh, because there would have been no way they would have broken him spiritually because he would have been forgiving each and every single person who was choosing to pick up and throw the stones which had led to his death. He would be forgiving every onlooker, every person that had ever done him harm throughout his life, and he would be praying for them, because that was the kind of person he was.

"Why are you laughing to yourself Moana?" asked Samira. "As if I need to ask, because I bet you are thinking the same as me."

When I told her, she laughed with me because that was exactly what she was thinking, and we both knew we were right. We reminded ourselves that he would have been at peace with it all, having zoned out and moved out of his physical body using the Muraqabah process of ascension meditation used by the Sufi's, a process both Samira and I had attempted. Neither of us had gotten anywhere close to being able to reach the ascension in its truest sense of mysticism like Faith had, but we had given it our all. I also knew the darker reason why he was so good at this ascension process, and not knowing whether Samira knew or not, I just kept quiet.

Had the ascension process been based on hard work and the highest expectations of ourselves, then we would have more than achieved it. Both of us being over achievers and incredibly harsh on ourselves, along with being so incredibly focused on what we were doing when working and intending with prayer and manifestation; but we were nowhere near the level of Muraqabah Faith was. He was a natural and had studied Al Ghazali and Rumi for many years. It came naturally to him, as did forgiveness and empathy.

"Remember when we were with him and how

everything seemed so light and peaceful, so easy and as if we were floating at all times?" Samira asked me.

"Hmmm…" a smile crossed my face again before I added, "And how when we read together we were transported to a different time and space, another realm. And how we'd discuss for hours what we had just read over mint tea and the ba'lawa I would get from Green Valley on every trip to Edgware Road."

"Oh, my goodness! Green Valley! Their sweets and bas'terma are just the best! The way you two would sit there and take off all the spices before eating the meat… it would take you ages to eat it." she laughed.

"Yeah but it was so good!"

We both fell silent again remembering how the three of us would devour books written by Martin Lings, Al Ghazali and Rumi, anything we could get our hands on about the mysticism of the great Sufi's, the aspect of Islaam we all connected to the most. It was almost our 'guilty secret' from all the others within our Islaamic community, and the more the 'Haram Police' would come out in force about some of our ideas, rejecting the very notion of Sufism as part of Islaam, the closer we all got.

So many times we had heard how the Sufis were a lost group of confused souls and how we were distorting Islaam, with many of the UK Muslims choosing to favour the strict cultural teachings of Suni Islaam from the Saudi's, propagated by the publishers Dar'el salaam – a publisher which would repel all of us in an instant just by looking at the book because we knew the distortion of the Holy Text of Qur'aan if ever there was any.

"So, what else do you know?" I asked. "And what are Teachers Without Borders doing about it?"

"Well, we know he had been working with the local village schools nearer to Islamabad, had been to Peshawar – because you know he had this thing about Peshawari naan bread with its almond and raisins." We both chuckled together again at the memories of always me and Faith debating the deliciousness of the Peshawari naan over the garlic naan, which is the one Samira favoured.

"He'd been helping teach in some of the schools and offering his help with the farming in the villages. He'd helped rebuild some of houses and local hospitals and had been absorbing the history of religious transitions between Hinduism, Buddhism and Islaam in the region. This is another theory about why he may have been targeted. He was touching on the British invasion and the religious corruption over the centuries.

From the phone calls we did get, he was well received by those in the smaller villages, and of course the kids loved him. He met many kindred spirits who lived Islaam rather than simply reciting scripture and not actually putting it all into action; mainly because many of them didn't read and were deeply connected to the earth and the natural world. He had been approached by the police a few times asking who he was, why he was there, and initially we put it down to the fact that he was a British tourist, but now…" Her voice trailed off and I heard more sobs on the other end of the line.

"Hey…" and then nothing more came out of my mouth. There was nothing more to say in this moment, just the need to hold space for each other and just be in the moments of grieving for our friend.

"As for Teachers Without Borders," Samira continued, "He felt too restricted with the places he had to go and what he was allowed to teach – and how he was allowed to teach, which I am sure sounds familiar to you."

"So, he was no longer working with them?" I clarified.

"No. He left them a couple of months ago, still working in the same kind of rural areas, but when he'd been in Pakistan for about six months, he felt confident enough to go it alone. He was still doing supply work for them every now and then, so there was still a good relationship between them, but no, he wasn't working with them, which is going to be used against him, no doubt."

I had to agree with her, it would be used against him, just as it had been used against others who had gone out to a country with Teachers Without Borders or with the British Council. Whilst the teachers were employed by them both, they were safe, but the moment they went freelance, they were on their own – and whatever happened to them was their own responsibility, which I could understand.

I then heard the words, "I'm hungry Marai. Where's Mama?" before hearing the sound of feet running towards me.

"Mama! Can we… what's the matter?" Salah said jumping on the bed and throwing his arms around me. "Marai, Mama's crying!" he shouted right in my ear as he held onto me tightly.

Marai came running through and the look on his face

when he saw mine made me see Faith. "Come on Salah, I'll make us some sandwiches."

"Ah cool! Can I have bas'terma and Puk? Yeah! Bas'terma and Puk! I want my khubz done on the flames… and I will do it!" declared Salah jumping off the bed.

With Salah already out of the door and on his way to the kitchen, Marai looked at me, blew me a kiss, and mouthed the words "I love you Mama" to which I mouthed the words "I love you too Baaba" back at him.

"Those boys," Samira said to me down the phone. "Marai tell you he loved you again habibiti?"

"You know he did. That boy, I am telling you… he is so good for my heart and Salah… always excited, cheeky, and ready to go."

"Sounds like someone else I know," replied Samira. "Apples, trees and all that jazz… isn't that what you say?" she teased.

"So, his parents know what's happened?" I said, confirming my understanding of the situation.

"Only the close family, that I know of, and I have only just found out because he was carrying my number and yours on him, and they couldn't get hold of you in Egypt. His cousin has confirmed it is him, but it won't be long until someone in Bradistan[1] finds out and tells them. I just hope I get there before anyone else does. You know how the Haram Police will take great pleasure in reciting hadeeth[2] and the different surahs[3] at his parent, brother, and sisters rather than offering them comfort and solace. And you know some of them will say this is what happens when we stray from the true path of Islaam."

"Yeah, well I am glad I am not there. You know how I

get when they all come out in force, especially the well-meaning do-gooders who are the most insensitive of them all… And that is coming from me, Little Miss Tactful over here."

This made Samira laugh because I had never been tactful since we had known each other, always saying the things which came to mind before they had finished forming in my own thought process, which was great in many ways, but not everyone was ready for the 'truth bombs' which I delivered on a regular basis.

"Hey, listen, I can hear the boys bickering over the amount of Puk which goes on their sandwiches, so I am going to go and sort them out before things get messy. Keep me updated, will you? And send my love to Haji[4] Chachu[5] and Haji Chachi.[6]"

"I will do habibiti. You take care of yourself out there. We are all worried about you too. Are things getting any better?"

I gave Samira a quick update on all things Egypt and the current state of play as we saw it. Updated her on how the teaching was going, how the boys were getting on in school, as well as my progress with my first book *Friday Bridge*. I told her how Abdullah was always out with the BBC covering the events as they unfolded, so it was mainly the boys and me in the apartment.

She gave me a brief update on how things were being reported back in England, which was so different to the reality, which was no surprise. She updated me on the local gatherings and told me how her studies were going, and that the other sisters missed me – especially my open house at iftar[7] time.

We then told each other we loved each other, promised to keep each other updated on news as soon as we heard anything and then said goodbye.

I sat and stared at the phone, hating it for bringing me this latest lot of sad news. It seemed the world was getting crazier by the minute… and then I heard the glass jar of PUK hit the floor and Marai shout, "Salah! Look at what you have done!" with Salah coming back with, "I didn't mean it! And it was nearly finished anyway. Where's the new jar?"

It was time to get my head straight and get into Mama mode and either save the boys from the broken glass on the floor … or the boys from each other.

---

1. The British term for Bradford due to the number of Pakistani's who live there. Bradford and Pakistan coming together to make Bradistan.
2. Something the majority of Muslims believe to be the words and actions of the Prophet Muhammad
3. The Arabic word for chapters in the Qur'aan
4. The name given to someone who has completed the Islaamic pilgrimage to Mecca known as Hajj.
5. The term of endearment for an uncle in Urdu
6. The term of endearment for an aunty in Urdu
7. Breaking of the fast-during Ramadhan

TWO

ALWAYS BELIEVE

Overhearing the conversation between my parents and my uncle, I was surprised by the way they were talking about the immigration 'situation' we were having in Britain, especially as they themselves were second generation immigrants.

They couldn't see how slowly they were falling for a rhetoric fed to them by the media and the hatred for the 'brown faces' and 'towel heads from those terrorist countries'. Not that my parents would ever use these particular phrases, but they too were starting to question the number of other Muslims and Pakistanis arriving in England. Where would they live? The drain on the schools and other resources, the tell-tale phrases used by the media and politicians.

Even though my parents were the kindest of people, they were starting to watch too much TV and read far too many of the tabloid newspapers, not the red tops with the naked women, but the *Daily Express* and the *Daily Mail* – two of the most racist newspapers in England, cleverly disguised as highbrow and liberal enough to not be Conservative, but Conservative enough to not be Labour or Liberal. Thankfully, they were not brainwashed just yet by the tell-a-vision and the system they had both grown up with during the sixties when immigration into Britain was at its peak. Their parents, my grandparents, had been some of the first Pakistanis to arrive in England, and they faced a weird kind of discrimination.

Weird because even though they were welcomed due to the need for workers in the factories, and the delicious aromas of exotic food which filled the air around towns and cities at mealtimes, many of the Brits were suspicious of what they didn't know about the rest of the world. An unconscious prejudice and fear which only got worse with the government agendas which the media fed to the people like a spoonful of sugar helping the medicine go down. This prejudice and fear, unbeknownst to my family, would unfold in some of the evilest of ways over the decades to come, tearing apart our family and the community they called home.

My grandparents, my mother's parents, were very well respected, as were most of the families who migrated to Britain in the beginning, and not only because they were helping to rebuild England after the war, but because many of the migrants who were given legal status right away were the families of those soldiers who had fought with the British in the army decades earlier.

Most of the brown faces now walking the streets of England were Punjabi Sikhs, others were the plantation children from the India tea regions, and then there were those like my family, the ones from Pakistan – the simple folk who chose not to embrace the British rule entirely, and the ones who still chose to follow the Qur'aan.

The Sikhs settled more in The Midlands around places such as Leicester, Coventry and Birmingham, with the Indians taking up residence in the larger hospital and more prestigious university locations such as Cambridge, Oxford and London, whilst the Pakistanis were the ones who had headed to Yorkshire in the north of England to start building and owning the textile industries using the silks they had brought with them from back home, opening up the corner shops from early in the morning to late at night, driving the taxis and serving the most delicious foods most English palettes had never experienced before.

Opening up restaurants for the community, especially those who had travelled with them from Pakistan, gave a strong sense of family to the local areas. "Families who eat together stay together, and that is good for our future" was something I heard my grandpa-daada say when I was younger and growing up. I always knew strength and a close bond with all aunties and uncles, and cousins in the neighbourhood.

Like the older, more polite of English traditions, the Pakistani's had a level of respect for their elders, so even if there was no shared blood, an older woman or man became an aunty and uncle. It was less formal than Mr or Mrs, or Sir or Madam, and gave the community a feeling of closeness, a bonding and a loyalty lost in most communities without it.

Everyone looked out for each other, dropped off meals or items of shopping. I grew up knowing to check on my neighbours, helping the elders with their gardening, or repairs on their homes, taking them to doctors when needed, and making sure they were greeted at the mosques and made comfortable to pray.

My grandpa-daada was the one who had the most intriguing faith out of all my family. He always told me to 'believe in the highest' but never told me what or how to believe, or who the highest was. He left me to choose for myself, to make my life and my beliefs my own because "When you make it your own, whatever that is, then you will always stay true to the path you were destined to travel upon." I loved my grandpa-daada, a name which I had given him when I was just a small boy making sense of the world of two languages. The languages from within my home where I lived with my parents, and the home I had outside of my family, the one with friend and their parents, and my teachers.

As I grew older, knowing two languages meant moving between two worlds, meant secrecy, and understanding more than others thought I did. It meant deeper connections with some people, and distance from others. Too Pakistani to be British and too British to be Pakistani. Always on the outside looking in on two worlds I didn't understand, and most of the time didn't want to be part of, especially when the kind of conversations I had just overheard were being had.

When Grandpa-daada passed away in 2009 I had just turned thirty, a pivotal point in my life, especially with his last words to me being "Ascension Babaji, it is the truest of paths and the highest connection you will ever have. Follow the teachings, question everything and let go of being in your body." Words which I never really understood until I was deep in the grieving process.

Most people didn't understand my grandpa-daada, thinking him eccentric and a dreamer, but as I questioned more about who I truly was as a human being, what my purpose for being here was, considering the bigger picture of things, the more each word in his last words took on a whole new meaning. A meaning which would transform into a beingness, with me as the creator of my life, a deeper connection with the almighty, a oneness, and a meaning which would eventually be fatal, and not just for me but for those who challenged the status quo, the ones who put faith into action.

The more I learned growing up with the weekly gatherings at the mosques for Friday Prayers, the nightly Qur'aan classes, the study of the history of Islam and the Arab countries, the more I fell in love with the teachings of Islam. With this falling in love came the questioning of those who preached, taught, and authored books on Islaam. Their views and understandings were different from mine, or Grandpa-daada's. They were not the loving, understanding or the 'living breathing' faith I had grown up learning from Grandpa-daada. My study of Arabic had shown me the translations in many of the books on Islam did not correctly match the English — or the Urdu.

The carefully chosen paragraphs to 'explain' Islaam to the non-Muslims, the narratives pushed in the various books was no different to the narratives pushed by governments and the media, only one was being used to spread fear and doubt about the brown faces and the 'bloody foreigners', whilst the other spread fear and doubt within oneself, and of course 'the infidel's.

The older I got, the more I began to question, the more of Grandpa-daada's treasured books I read. There were few, but the ones he had mentioned this 'higher self', this ascension, and the worlds beyond. My mother Noor, and father Hani, would read endlessly, but my youngest sister Amina, hardly ever read, even though it was a direct instruction in the Qur'aan. My parents respected my love of reading, but they did not like me reading books on other religions, mysticism, and paganism as much as I did. My older sister Shaista read a lot of fiction and her study books, but even she wasn't a lover of books like I was. I asked too many questions, and liked to discuss the concepts I was reading about. My family couldn't answer my questions and would sometimes ask me to stop discussing certain subjects, such as the shamanism and witchcraft of other faiths. "It will bring the devil and evil spirits to our door!" my mother once said. This reaction made me miss Grandpa-daada even more because we would discuss the books, go off on tangents, discussing, dissecting, and dissolving ideas and concepts together.

Educated my parents may have been, but cultural beliefs and indoctrination always ran deeper, no matter the nationality and faith. Too afraid to lose their Pakistani heritage, and too afraid to not embrace the British way of life meant levels of fear collided within in the most paradoxical of ways.

My questions often infuriated our local Imam, so much so he would visit my parents and tell them I was on the edge of losing my faith altogether. My parents knew this to be untrue, and my father warned me about asking so many questions in the Qur'aan classes which contradicted and showed the ignorance of the Imam. I soon became disillusioned with the classes and would write down all my questions, so when I returned home, I could look for the answers myself in books.

Hearing Grandpa-daada tell me I was good and holy, to keep studying, to keep asking the questions people didn't want me to ask, spurred me on. His words gave me the strength I needed to withstand the loneliness which would creep up on me. A loneliness which came from being so fascinated with religion that other kids thought I was 'not cool enough' or 'too radical' that the 'pious kids' were told to stay away from me for the fear their parents had that I would 'lead them astray.' The isolation grew, and with it grew a deeper faith in myself and a deeper love of understanding this religion that was meant for all of humanity, for all of time.

In my teens I observed the hypocrisy and double standards in pretty much every aspect of my life. Adults saying one thing and then doing the other, telling us to not argue and then arguing – or rather debating around the dinner table. At the dinner table it was a blend of love, laughter and never one of aggression, but watching how they would get deal with each other on an individual basis away from prying eyes, the frustration of life's circumstances heavy on their shoulders, I wondered if these adults truly did believe in everything they said.

I would hear my parents, uncles, and aunties – pretty

much any adult to be honest – repeating "Everything happens for a reason" and that "Allah is the All-knowing, All-powerful and most merciful, trust Him," but then getting so anxious all the time. If they genuinely believed the words which were written in the Qur'aan, then surely they wouldn't be anxious?

And if we were all equal in the eyes of Allah, why did they try and prove themselves to others, expressing themselves to be above, or inferior to, others?

There were some families who were not clean and tidy in their appearances, their gardens, and their homes, and yet to be clean is an act of worship. There were others who did not read or achieve wisdom, so with the first word in the Qur'aan being 'ikra' which means 'read', and the second most used word in the Qur'aan being 'ilm' meaning 'wisdom' I was surprised there was not more reading and seeking of knowledge being done.

Then there was the aspect of the body being a trust from Allah, along with the planet, and how no one seemed to be taking care of their heath. Smoking, eating lots of sugar, as well as putting loads of sugar in their chai tea, rotting their teeth with every mouthful.

I would look at the way in which so many of the women around me were 'softer' when in social circles with their husbands, and yet when my mama-gi was with her female friends, they would be talking non-stop offering each other opinions and advice on everything, discussing what was going on in the news and laughing loudly with each other.

In the Qur'aan it says, "Love your mother first, second,

third and then your father" and yet mothers were taken advantage of hourly, not just daily, but every hour of the day. They were put upon by the men in the families, including the sons. They were prevented from working a job outside of the home, and many of the women I knew were not educated in anything other than serving the family by cooking and cleaning. How is this loving the power of a woman? Or honouring her in all of who she is? How is this wisdom? And how did this lack of respect for women in our Pakistani culture blend or allow our women to integrate into the British society my grandpa-daada and others like him, had chosen as their home?

My mother was one of the luckier ones, and she knew it. My father knew my mother was smarter than he was, knew she was stronger than he was in mind, emotion, and faith. He would always seek her counsel on everything he did. He never raised his voice or a hand to her like some of the fathers of my friends did, and so I always had a profound respect for my father.

Of all the families living in our community in Bradford, my family were one of the most respected, something which made me proud of who I was. I was proud of my family name, of the kindness my parents and grandpa-daada showed others. It showed me how being kind and supportive of others, always helping where we could, and having great manners, was the best way to be.

The ruling in Islam of always thinking of seven reasons why someone is the way they are, or behaving in a way they do, and if you can think of seven, think of another seven, until you have thought of so many reasons you have gained compassion and love for the person, was something instilled within me and my brother every time we got frustrated or upset with one another.

My brother Malak and I were quite different. I was always in my books, he was always climbing trees and walls, being outside physically active. We would share our adventures with each other at the end of each day as we lay in bed, his of how amazing he felt inside of his body and how cool it was to be able to climb so many things. I would share the adventures of knowledge with him I had gained from reading and questioning, excited by all his questions and observations. We were inseparable in this way, deeply connected and one half of the other, even though we were born two years apart.

Our family was unusual in the way there were only four siblings, two girls and two boys, as most of the Pakistani families had five or six children, a belief that the more children you had the more chance of some of them surviving and being able to take care of each other the older we all got. The truth was, looking at the older siblings in families in the community, the older they got the more divided they were as some became increasingly British, whilst others dug deeper into the culture of a Pakistan they had never visited, just one they had created in their mind from the stories told by the elders. The Pakistan which had been created of only the good memories, and none of the bad memories for fear of losing the love of home and country.

Malak and I spurred each other on. We motivated and challenged each other, making us not only inseparable, but also stronger in our individual selves. We were a force to be reckoned with, in discussions, in solidarity and within our community. We were rascals of opposite ends of the scale which endeared us to others, whilst also alienating us in ways which we would not realise, or understand, until later in life.

THREE
THE HA'RAAM POLICE

That night after the boys had gone to bed, I thought back to the very first time I had met Faith. The smiles and the tears flowed in equal measure, and not just because a few months earlier my friend Amira had died, but because I remembered just how Faith made me question so much about the life I had created for my boys by being part of a multicultural family.

He made me question whether I had unconsciously made their life so much harder by simply being open minded and welcoming of all cultures, ethnicities, and faiths. I knew the world needed more open-hearted people – accepting, and welcoming of one another – but falling in love with Abdullah was so easy and I believed he would be a great dad. His ethnicity and faith didn't come into it, he was just another great human being.

Lying there on the couch waiting for Abdullah I drifted off into a world of memories of Faith and how we had connected all those years before at one of the more 'enlightened' Islaamic events in England.

Remembering his first words to me, *You know, you really should be in the main hall praying with everyone else...* I chuckled to myself. Always mimicking the ha'raam police to spark a conversation with someone but doing it in such a playful way that he never offended people, not even the hardcore Salafis and Wahabis could resist his cheekiness.

It was a moment of connection with a 'brother' which was more like meeting myself, or one of my male friends from the rave scene: completely easy, with fun filled, deep conversations down the rabbit hole within moments of meeting. There was no small talk, just a deep dive into ideas, philosophies, and paradoxes.

His desire to explore ideas, concepts and engage with others to deepen both his understanding of faith and humanity, and the person he was conversing with often left him deflated and disillusioned due to the strict or prejudiced ideas they had about religion, and Islaam.

For both me and Faith we knew we were all Divine beings. In each of the holy texts it stated in one way or another that God breathed life into us, fashioned us from clay and that He was closer to us than our jugular vein, so logically we were God, Allah, and any other name any of us chose to use to describe the higher entity or force we all prayed to.

A view which did not go down well with the majority of others who thought we were infidels and blasphemous in our ideas.

Hearing those first words of Faith coming from behind me at the Ramadan retreat, I'd turned around with my eyebrows raised in defiance and disregard for whoever it was who had just chosen to tell me what to do, ready to be on the defence, but was taken aback by the kind, smiling, and cheeky look on the man's face.

Remembering his face in my mind's eye was all it took for me to unleash the tears I had been holding back whilst the boys were awake.

My dear friend killed in such a horrendous way. It didn't make any sense, but sadly, it made perfect sense. He was challenging all the cultural dogma, and he was 'one of the treacherous infidels who masqueraded as a Muslim leading the youth astray'. He represented the ultimate treason in the eyes of those who didn't have the capacity to think beyond what the local Imam had instilled within them during all the Friday prayers. The fear of questioning, of challenging what was 'reported', of connecting the dots, of thinking for themselves, and of going beyond the local mosque.

Allowing the tears to fall, I remembered how the rest of the conversation had played out and then started smiling. The playful banter had started immediately between us, and as I replayed our first conversation over in my mind, I got up off the couch and made his favourite tea of mint, cinnamon, cloves, nutmeg, and star anise – with milk and a dash of honey just the way he liked it.

With the memories cascading through my mind, I held the mug as if I were holding onto the memories so they would never fade away. The sweet tea soothed me on many levels, but as someone who is unused to sweet tea, I took my time drinking it.

The gratitude I felt to have met this magical soul, to have grown in faith and heightened awareness of what it meant to be a Sufi meant the world to me. Abdullah was dismissive of the Sufis, as were most of the Muslims I met. Even the more liberal and enlightened Muslims I'd met around the world didn't mention Sufism. It was regarded as 'more of a Western hippie thing' by those who were 'born Muslims'. Faith, Samira – another 'hippie infidel' friend – and I often referred to it in laughter as 'the gateway drug' to Islaam, just without the negative stereotypes 'proper efnik' Muslims experienced.

I placed the tea on the coffee table and lay back and just allowed the memories to flow, treasuring each and every encounter, each event we'd attended, each book we'd read and discussed, and each meal we had made and eaten together.

If he'd lived closer, I am sure he would have moved into my spare room. He was great with the boys when they were younger, always bringing them a treat of Pakistani Gold, also known as Carrot Halwa or Gajar al Halwa. It was made by his mum using grated carrot, coconut milk, honey, almonds, and raisins, although most Pakistanis would use cow's milk, Haji Chachi would only use the coconut milk. "Makes it healthy" she would say.

Returning back to the memories of our first meeting I remembered making him laugh, blush and a little envious about me being a woman when I'd replied to his cheeky comment telling me I should be praying.

"If that is true for me, then it must also be true for you, especially because as a woman I could be on a period and so therefore by the blessing of Allah, I get a holiday from praying."

"A holiday hey? Interesting take on it. And yes, probably, but I pray all the time and I don't really want to be lectured by the Imam," came the same cheeky tone of voice, but this time with a tone of resignation and boredom dancing within it.

I had known exactly what he meant. The way many Imams lectured and chastised rather than invited reflection and discussion, so our belief and faith could be deepened and put into practice was so off-putting. The Imams who invited reflection and discussion always had a full house on fridays and were loved by many everywhere; and when attending Friday Prayers hosted by these Imams you would see the most diversity in the Ummah – the word we used instead of congregation or community.

The longer we spoke, the more we joked and laughed about how we would be frowned upon due to the absurdity of how it was haram for us to be speaking with each other in the eyes of others. With so many 'brothers and sisters' unwilling to speak with one another because they had been fed with the fear that they would become possessed by the devil, the third person in the room. The devil would infiltrate their minds with inappropriate thoughts leaving them wanting to rip each other's clothes off at any given moment – or worse still, being tempted into hot and frenzied sexual fornication right there in the moment – because no one had any self-control at all, regardless of how many hours and days they fasted for.

"So why are you not fighting your way to be at the

front of the prayer congregation to prove how pious you are?" he asked.

"Oooo someone's got some issues with the ummah," I laughed. "And sit down, you make the place look untidy."

"Yeah, you could say that. I mean look around you, all the women doing their best to be more pious in their covering up than the next 'sister', bringing dishes more elaborate or in greater quantity than the others, and changing their names to be the most pious, most religious, most Pakistani out of the rest of them." His head was lowered now, and a sadness had taken over.

I sat smiling to myself because I understood and agreed with him in all he was saying. I was done with all the Muslim events and social gatherings, had been for a long time. The Islamic Awareness Week was nothing more than a Pakistani Awareness Week and many of those who were now reverts, those who have chosen to 'return' to Islam rather than continuing in 'a state of the infidel' were becoming increasingly Pakistani than they were becoming Muslim. Many had little to no historical knowledge and were not willing to even question the 'hadith'[1] and if I was given one more dish of curry at an Islamic event, I was likely to throw it at the person giving it to me.

So yes, I understood where this guy was coming from.

"You get it, don't you?" he said.

"Yes, I do," I replied.

"And that's why you are out here by yourself and have been sat observing what is going on more than taking part in the event." He stated more than he asked.

"That would be correct, plus I have come to realise that just because we all share the same title 'Muslim' we couldn't be more different if we tried. None of the women here make me even want to go and speak with them. The way they interact with each other, the way they don't play with their kids, the way they are speaking about piety all the time, it just does my head in. I have been ready to go for hours, and I have only been here since yesterday." I vented with a resignation and a breath that needed releasing.

"Wow, someone else willing to speak these truths," he laughed. "My name is Faith by the way, nice to meet you Moana."

I was taken aback by the fact he had called me by my name.

"You seem surprised I know your name."

"Yes, I am."

"Well, you are pretty famous in these circles you know. Everyone here saw the documentary you made with Channel 4 and read the article in *Emel Magazine*. Why do you think so many of the more pious sisters avoid you and do not even approach you?" He asked.

"Probably because I am wearing combats and trainers, with an African/hip hop bandana, and have a long-sleeved t-shirt on?" I said, knowing full well I was far to 'Western' in my style for the gallabiyah wearing 'holier than thou' sisterhood that was forever present at any and all of the Islamic events I had attended.

The bright pink full-length skirts and a white suit jacket, with a bright pink headscarf tied in the African bandana style I wore for the Channel 4 series was just too rebellious for 99% of the 'sisters' who I came across.

"Ha! I know you don't believe that. You know it is

because you challenge everything they have allowed themselves to believe. You know they have fallen for the dogmatic cultural diatribe rather than knowing that Islam is a religion for all people for all of time, and that we don't have to change our nationality or our names to become a Muslim. And I know you know this, because I have heard you speak on many occasions." Faith responded with such force and certainty even I was taken aback.

I couldn't help but smile and feel a little uncomfortable that my reach in the community had become bigger than I had allowed myself to realise. Here was a perfect stranger who had seen me speak, appear on TV and in magazines speaking on the very topics we were discussing right now. Part of me was happy to have met someone who had seen me on these stages and platforms, but a part of me felt a little unprepared for it too.

"Yeah, and I also know that just us having this conversation amounts to backbiting and judging others without knowing them and their journey. Which is why I speak out and question everything publicly, so those who need another perspective rather than the dogma they have been fed, can then choose to explore, and question deeper for themselves," I replied.

"Do you think they will though? Honestly? I doubt it. They have been taught to not question the faith…"

"Even though it clearly states in Surah Bakara that we must question everything and not follow our forefathers blindly." We both said in unison, which made us both laugh and smile at one another.

"You know you are not allowed to smile at me because I am a man. And you are not allowed to invite me to sit with you or have a conversation with me whilst we are alone here in this vast dining hall," Faith said, adding another layer of the cultural brainwashing we were both against.

"So, if you are not happy being here, why are you here?" I asked him out of curiosity.

"Because even though I know this is what it will be like, I also have this hope that I will be proven wrong about it all. I hope that just one year this event will have so many free thinkers and truly enlightened Muslims, on their way to being an Ihsaan[2], that I will be so surprised and fall in love with the community. But here I am, in my fifth year here and more pissed off by the event than ever. It just gets more and more Pakistani every year," he replied with a real sadness and disappointment in his voice that was hard to ignore and upsetting to hear.

He sat in silence for a few moments, his head down and a resigned sadness surrounding him. Looking at him I saw someone who was deeply dissatisfied and frustrated, as well as alone in the way in which he saw the world.

Dressed in his jeans, with a pair of Adidas trainers, a regular t-shirt and clean-shaven baby face, you wouldn't know this young lad was a Muslim. And I liked that about him. After all, our faith was between us as individuals and Allah, not us and everyone else. It was the way in which we practiced our faith, rather than how many verses of the Qur'aan we could recite flawlessly. Memorising something didn't mean you understood the context, it just meant that you had spent many hours, days, weeks, months and even years reading, reciting, and committing to memory passages which could be recalled at any given moment. To me this wasn't faith, and it appeared that Faith also felt the same way.

"How old are you, Faith?" I asked.

"Twenty-six. Why?" He replied.

"Just wondered. You seem to want to be anywhere but here, so why are you here? Why are you not with friends elsewhere? Not that age has anything to do with it, but why are you here instead of doing something more productive with your time? And your life?"

"I have been asking myself the same questions to be honest with you. I also don't have many friends – not that I want sympathy, mind you – but for a Pakistani lad there are almost certainly only two options for me: 1) Become a devout and unquestioning servant of Allah – i.e. slave to cultural dogma, attending mosque every day whilst wearing traditional Pakistani clothes and eating nothing but curry, whilst also carrying prayer beads and a Qur'aan with me at all times to prove to my family and community that I am a devout and practising Muslim, or 2) Rebel against all of that by smoking pot and hanging out with other rebels on the street corners or racing our pimped out Golf GTI 'in-nit' with vulgar rap music blasting from our car speakers. Neither option appeals to me."

The depth of sadness he said all of this with made the mother in me want to hold him tight and tell him everything would be all right. He wasn't my son though, and even touching him would have been the biggest scandal to happen at the Ramadhan Retreat since the annual event had begun a few years before.

"If you are asking yourself these questions, then why are you not answering them? Or praying, meditating, allowing the answer to come to you? Because the thing is, you already know what you need to do," I responded. "And by the way, they are some pretty black and white stereotypes you have there."

"Tell me I am wrong about the stereotypes," he came back challenging me. "Tell me what else there is for me to identify with, when I don't identify with either. It's like knowing I am British and English, and also South Asian and Pakistani. I identify with them all, but none of them all at the same time."

"You identify with yourself, and what you know to be true."

He smiled and nodded, and then looked out the window at the big open grass field where my boys were playing together on the bouncy castle which had been set up. I'd been sat watching them whilst having five minutes peace to enjoy a cup of tea.

Things had been pretty hectic over the last few months, and I was in the process of packing up our home to move to Egypt. My friend Amira was with the boys and loving every last moment she could get with them.

"Have you met Amira? The lady out there with my boys?" I asked Faith.

"No, why?" he asked.

"You'd like her. A fiery Scottish woman who calls it like we do. And yet, see what she is wearing. The traditional black gallabiyah with the floral headscarf tied the traditional Arabic way. Are you not allowing the stereotypes to block you from meeting others who think like we do?" I asked him.

"I take your point, and yes, I probably wouldn't have

approached her. Not just because of what she is wearing, but because she is an older lady. We just don't do that sort of thing in my culture," he responded.

"And which culture is that?" I asked him. "The British culture you have which leads you to wear the clothes you are wearing and the culture in which you have lived in, been to school in and currently work in, or the Pakistani culture which you obviously have issues with?"

"Touché!" He laughed. "I get your point."

"Good, now come on outside and meet her, and my boys. Their names are Salah and Marai."

"Again, with the Arabic names, and not religious Islamic names. Why?"

"Because it is not for me to tell my sons what faith they will have. They have to choose it for themselves. They have to discover what works and doesn't work for them. Like I did, and like you are doing. I don't think it is right to trap a child into the beliefs we as parents hold by giving them a religious name. Who I am to have that much control over the destiny of my child. I am their mother, not their dictator. Now come on, it's Mama time for me, so if you want to continue the conversation, it's time for us to move outside… before the Haram Police stop praying and come out here with disapproving eyes."

---

1. sayings and practices of the Prophet Mohammed
2. The highest level of faith possible in Islaam

FOUR

BECOMING PART OF THE FAMILY

"You really are different to the rest, aren't you? It is so nice talking with you and I wish more parents thought the same way as you do. Are you sure it is okay to join you and your sons?" Faith shyly asked, which was very different to the young confident man who had walked up behind me less than twenty minutes before.

"I wouldn't have invited you if it weren't. And no, I am not like the others, nor will I be. God made me the way I am for a reason and so to not be who I am, is a dishonour to God, is it not?" I replied, getting up from my seat and making my way over to the kitchen to return my mug. "So, are you coming then or not?"

"Yes, I would like that. Thank you."

We made our way over to the bouncy castle continuing the conversation. Having watched this young man go from the confident one who had approached me, believing I was famous and still choosing to challenge me, to seeing him soften and become unsure of himself and who he was, which made me look at my own boys differently. It was an interesting shift to witness, especially as others were the reverse: nervous upon approaching, and confident when they realised I was just like them, only with a different career choice.

Were my boys going to grow up with the same identity crisis this young man was obviously experiencing?

Was having me as a mother, someone who called out the tribal diatribe and rhetoric going to have a positive or negative impact on their own views of religion?

And did I actually want my boys to follow a religion or simply have a strong faith in this higher energetic life force, this entity, this incredible power, whatever it was?

Faith was also beginning to question whether he wanted to be part of a religion and identify as a Muslim, because not only did he not relate to other Muslims, other than a few friends, but he was having identity issues as well. He may not have said so in as many words, but it was becoming increasingly obvious as I watched and processed what he had already shared with me. And I understood this on many levels because the more I was reading the Qur'aan, the more Arabic I spoke, read, and understood, the less connected to the Islamic community I felt.

Walking over to the boys, I asked Faith about where he thought his journey would take him, and if he had considered the higher levels of consciousness and mysticism – or, as the mainstream called it – Sufism. There were very few of those around in England, and I was hoping to learn more when the boys and I finally moved to Egypt by meeting more Sufis.

Much like Faith, I was hoping that each year I attended the Ramadhan Retreat, something would ignite a connection, not in my faith – we both had that in vast amounts, but in religion. Would embarking on the deeper spiritual elements of Islaam be any different? Or would it be more of the same – Sufis by name, but not by practice?

It was like Faith and I were reading each other's thoughts, recognising within each other the doubts, the desire for more clarity and the disillusion we felt for the national and global narratives, as well as the community events which passed themselves off as Islamic, but really had nothing to do with Islam, and more to do with outdoing one another's piousness, and the Pakistani integration into British society.

We were snapped out of our thoughts by the cheery voice of my friend Amira. "As salaam alaykum Hassan!"

"Wa alaykum as salaam Amira, the name is Faith though," he replied.

"Ock, it may well be, but you are Hassan too!" laughed my short Scottish friend Amira, with the most alive face and eyes I had seen of any of my Muslim sisters.

"Oh! Yes, I see. Thank you, Auntie!" laughed Faith, instantly relaxing in Amira's presence.

"Oh, bless you lad, less of Auntie, you make me feel old. Amira, please," she said turning to me. "These wee bairns are getting tired, and I am not interested in staying any longer. Already bored out of this wee and grand body of mine. Shall we be heading home?"

"I am more than happy to, if you are," I replied. "Where do you live Faith?"

"Oh, I live up in none other than Bradistan, hence the stereotypes I mentioned earlier."

"Well, if you are happy to leave with us, then come on

over for dinner, the more the merrier, hey boys?" said Amira as she got the boys ready for heading home. "First the toilets, we don't want any stops on the way back, unless it's me in my old age," she laughed.

"You're crazy Aunty Amira!" cackled Salah. "And let's get pizza!"

"Pizza! Pizza! Pizza!" cheered both Salah and Marai jumping up and down with their arms in the air.

"If that's okay, that would be great, thank you," Faith said with that shyness that kept peeking through his eyes and wrapping him up in its wake. "If you don't mind, I would like to go and tell my cousins I will be heading back to Sheffield with you and then getting the train back."

"No worries. Do what you have to do. Amira and the boys will be a good fifteen minutes anyway, and knowing Amira, she will be getting some of those lovely pakoras and bhajis for snacks on the way," I replied.

Twenty minutes later we were all in the car leaving the Ramadhan Retreat and heading for sanity back in Sheffield, via Pizza Hut to collect three large pizzas because the boys had already decided they wanted pizza for breakfast the next morning.

On the way back to Sheffield Amira quizzed Faith on his life in 'Bradistan' – the Pakistani Bradford, hence the name 'Bradistan'. She quizzed him on how long his family had been in Bradford, whether his parents spoke any English, and when he answered he was the third generation of his family to be in England and that his parents were both English speakers, as were his siblings, things started to become a lot clearer to both Amira and me.

Here we had a young lad whose faith told him he had to integrate into the land of his home, obey the laws of the land and which had the Arabic word for 'wisdom' – ilm – mentioned more in the Qur'aan than charity, and the first word of the Holy text being 'Ikra' – which meant 'read' – and both his parents, even though second generation, both spoke English.

His mother did part-time work, and both his sisters were defying and breaking all rules of the local community. His youngest sister had even chosen to leave home for her job and had her own independence, her own money and lived life the way she wanted to – without hijaab. He had remained at home so he could study and support his mother, a woman who had been deeply upset by her youngest daughter leaving the family home to live by herself.

Amira, ever the inquisitor, also found out that Faith had also chosen to become a youth worker so he could help the younger generations become stronger in faith, questioning the rhetoric and dogma that was handed down every friday during Friday Prayers at the mosque. He wanted to be the person who was there for all those who thought deeper, questioned everything, and wanted to live their faith on their own terms, rather than having to live a disjointed life of the life their parents wanted them to live.

"You're walking a path few are willing to travel young man, and I think you are brave. You have a lot to lose, but you also have a lot to gain in terms of your own inner peace. And you couldn't be connected with someone better. Moana here will see you right." Hearing my friend say these words about me, and the journey Faith was on, reminded me of the way others saw me. She knew the struggles I had been having, and we could both see that Faith was struggling with very much the same issues.

People had become so focused on scripture, on belonging to a religion and a community, that they had forgotten about putting faith into action. Ego was taking over, along with aspects of 'Keeping up with the Jones'', or as Faith liked to put it 'Keeping up with the Khan's'.

Our faith had been born out of a love for nature, curiosity, and connection, whereas so many around us were either unconscious of choice, or afraid to question their parents, ethnicity, and community. A Muslim by choice was a rarity, and one of the reasons so many 'born Muslims' admired us reverts so much was because we had learnt so much about the faith, had questioned who we were, what we believed and where we belonged in life, as well as what we wanted to achieve in life, something so many of them were afraid to do because they had always been taught to not question their parents, the Imam's and certainly not question the religion – that was simply blasphemous and equated the person questioning to an infidel; and in the local and wider community, one just didn't question Islam.

Faith, and I, had other ideas. We both believed the more we questioned the religion, the Qur'aan the deeper our faith became, the more answers we gained, and the more enlightened we became.

Asking the questions led us to study history, geography, the sciences, and human nature, gathering all the knowledge we were gaining into a deeper pot of knowledge which only strengthened our faith, but weakened our need to belong to a religion.

A religion, like them all, which had been created by man, and not just one man, but a collective, and not the messengers themselves: but outside forces, corrupted the beauty and intentions of the initial messages. The goodness channelled through the messages, the peace and harmony they were meant to bring wouldn't bring the control the power hungry wanted. The messages wouldn't bring the fear or disruption needed to keep them in power; they would only bring forgiveness, love, and collaboration between the people, and that would never be a good thing for those who wanted control.

FIVE

THE STRUGGLE IS REAL

A week after our first meeting, Faith and I jumped on a Skype call.

"'Come on Babaji, it's time to go to mosque. You'll be late.' It's all I would hear from my mother growing up, whether it was Qur'aan class twice a week after school, Friday prayers or the Islaamic version of the Christian Sunday School. Life in England seemed to revolve around us all going to mosque to prove we were still Muslim enough, just because we lived in England. My cousin Zair, who was still living in Pakistan, would laugh when he heard the amount of time British Pakistanis attended mosque.

'It's so confusing Zair. It's like they are all scared of me rejecting who they are and what they believe in, and yet pushing me to challenge the old ways and educate myself. Sometimes when I talk of the concepts I am learning, they remind me of their narrative of life, which shows me they are not concerned or even aware of how that would lead me to losing who I am; and then the next day they are embracing the ideas I present to them.'

'They are slowly learning from you Faith, and the ideas and concepts you present to them are making sense the more you drip feed your thoughts to them. Keep doing it Chacha Zad, you are making a positive difference… even in my life. I learn from you too, don't forget that. It is challenging, and sometimes I don't like what you say, but we are young. It is easier for us to break down the narratives we are being taught because we do not have decades of programming within us. Be patient with them, and yourself Chacha-Zad. Patience is holy, is it not?'

'I know, Zair, but it does my head in how so many Muslims, and other believers think that we can only worship the Almighty by walking inside a building and putting coins in a collection box. The entire world is a mosque, and we can pray anywhere, by ourselves or in a community. It's not like Allah only sees us in the bloody mosque, is it?' I would rage about this at my cousin, who was the only family member, other than Grandpa-daada, who I felt totally at ease saying these things to.

'Chacha, you know you could always move out of the family home and get a job down south. And really? Bloody mosque? That's not very politically correct now, is it?' he would laugh. 'And I understand your love of praying outside. When we have been working out in the fields or been out to town, we often pray together out in the garden for Maghrib and Isha' prayer. The feeling of the breeze on our faces, the smell of the plants and the soil… and the cow pats, they all add to the sense that we are all connected with one another to the Almighty Allah.'

'You have now lost the plot my friend!' I would tell him laughing. 'You know that I can't leave the family home until I am married – can you imagine the shame?! And exactly my point! Being outside when praying brings such a depth of tranquillity to our prayers, and yet all people seem to want is the sound of a fan or air conditioning unit, the buzz of electricity, and the smell of each other – which to be honest with you Chacha zad, has made me understand what the Brits mean when they say you can smell a Pakistani coming – we all smell of last night's curry, and every curry we have ever eaten!'

Laughing and bantering with him always made me feel like I needed to visit him straight away, and it was after this conversation that the seed of moving out for a job in the 'big smoke' took root, but I knew the 'big smoke' wouldn't be London, it would be a big city back home in Pakistan, but for an international firm. The only way to overcome the shame of leaving the family home was to get a prestigious corporate job in London and then get transferred to Pakistan, so that became my focus. As well as the day I would arrive in Pakistan to visit Chacha zad, and the rest of the family.

I'd always wanted to learn more about why my grandpa-Dadda had left and how Pakistani Muslims practised Islaam in Pakistan and didn't know what was really stopping me. I kept asking myself if life was really that different, or just my cousin Zair's point of view. As well as asking if life really was so difficult in Pakistan, which is why so many left. And did they have more faith or more religion 'back home in Pakistan' where the virtues of Islaam were stronger?

My cousin and I would talk for hours, like you and I are now doing Moana, and it would always leave me with more questions than answers. The discrepancy between the Qur'aan and the way in which Pakistani's practiced their faith showed me how important it was for me to deepen my understanding of Arabic. I knew the basics and could converse with my Arabian friends to a basic level of discussion, but to learn the language of the Qur'aan Fusha would be the ideal. I needed to become fluent. Little did I know this would alienate me from my family and community even more because they didn't understand the subtleties of the teachings within the Qur'aan, and it is when I finally understood why Islaam was so different the world over. Having asked myself if I understood the teachings properly for many years, I was able to correct my understandings, question more, and the more I questioned, the more rage I would face from my parents and those who followed blindly, which we are told not to do – in black and white – in the second chapter of the Qur'aan.

I think the saddest thing for me was learning of the way in which the women were treated as baby makers and less than second class citizens; and in some tribes my Chacha zad spoke of the women were treated worse than the chickens and goats in their back yards. There was no way I would want my mother or sisters to be treated in this way, any woman in fact. This dangerous misunderstanding of the Qur'aan made me even more determined to visit Pakistan, to support my female cousins, aunties, and sisters in Islaam.

Knowing women were not allowed to be educated in most suburbs and villages in Pakistan, with the lucky ones only being educated to the ages of fourteen and fifteen, if they were lucky, didn't sit well with me. Especially knowing how education benefitted the whole of society. Knowing girls didn't receive an education at all in remote villages, only the boys to a basic level, made me view my mother in a whole new light. She was educated because she grew up in England, and she was adamant my sisters would also be educated; one of the main reasons my grandparents came to England. My family were pioneers in many ways, and I knew if I could get them to see me and my dream through their eyes, the eyes of Grandpa-daada, then this would be the way I would get their support... even if it meant moving so far away from them all.

Sitting down together over dinner was the easy part, so I just came out and told them that I was going to get a job in London for a multinational with the end goal of moving to Pakistan to do some charity work, which wasn't exactly a lie, but it wasn't exactly the full truth either.

I had discovered an organisation called Teachers Without Borders and I had already done the research to find out what was needed. It was a multinational, and I did have to attend some seminars in London and some training courses on the organisations, but it wasn't the multinational firm my father was hoping I would be joining. He had his heart set on my joining a firm such as Deloitte and Touche, or PWC ... which I was not qualified for, but still, these company names were recognised in big business so had more prestige for him to name drop with his friends.

My mother's reaction was unexpected, and the look of love and pride on her face when I told her I was going into teaching in remote areas of Pakistan had brought her almost to tears with joy. 'Oh Babaji! This is wonderful news! You know Grandpa-daada would be so proud of you. You are the circle of life he always talked about. Sowing the seeds of education that he had sowed within us back home in Pakistan. Masha'Allah, Alhamdu'lilah! Allah has blessed us all with this choice.'

'When do you leave?' was the first question my father asked me.

'Why you want to get rid of him so quickly?!' my mother answered quickly with a bite to her words.

'No, my love, I just want to help him prepare himself properly. He has made me proud with this choice of his, and now it is our job to make sure he knows what he is getting himself in for, and to support him by making contacts back home. When we know when he is due to leave, family can be there waiting for him, making plans to host him and such like… before he goes off with this excellent organisation,' my father replied, taking my mother's hand in his and speaking so softly towards her.

Honestly, the love my father had for my mother was something else. I have never seen any man love a woman the way my father loved my mother. It was both comforting and confronting at the same time because as children we knew we had a strong and close, loving family, but we also knew a love like theirs didn't come along very often, or so we were told.

So often we had heard men shouting at their wives and children along the street, and my mother spoke in hushed tones to my father about such-and-such an aunty who was beaten by her husband when my father found her sad and praying for her fellow sisters in Islaam. 'These men do not know how to love a woman like you do my love. They mark their woman with bruises on their bodies and fear in their hearts and minds.'

My father would always respond with, 'Let's pray for them my love and ask Allah to show them the way.'

They never knew I would spy on them through the gap in the doorway or stand outside their bedroom door hearing my mother in tears as she retold my father of the horrors the aunties in the local area had experienced. Recounting these times was also a driver for me to make this choice. How could I dishonour my grandpa-daada and my baba-gi by allowing my sisters in Islaam back home in Pakistan to go without education and become enlightened and empowered like my mother and sisters.

My sister Shaista looked at me with curiosity, whilst Amina asked me what subject I would be teaching, fully in the belief that it would be English literature. Malak continued eating whilst my parents discussed the logistics. Once he had finished eating, he put his hand up to high five me and said, 'Dude, this is great news. I can now have our room all to myself. Lots of girls over, smoking weed....' To which we all started laughing, including Mama-Gi and Baba-Gi...

'There will be no girls in your room Malak,' my father corrected.

'Cool, so weed is alright then?' replied Malak, leaving Amina nearly choking on her mouthful of lassi, and Shaista snorting out her water.

Sharing this dream went better than I ever thought it would, and it was wonderful to have the support of all of them. Chacha zad was of course delighted when I told him how things had gone, and if I had left plans to him in

Pakistan, I would never have left his side. I had to remind him many times that I was not there to party with him and find a bride along the way. I was there to teach 'and un-doctrinate the masses over here in this deprived and antiquated country of your ancestors' he would joke; sometimes I wasn't sure if he were joking or not, but I couldn't let that stop me.

The only way I would find out if he were joking or not was to spend time with him in amongst his friends and the family back home. Was he the same person I knew, loved, and respected on the phone, or a completely different person when surrounded by the local community? Only time would tell, and the closer my departure for Pakistan got, the more apprehensive I became. This wasn't just a holiday to visit family. This was a whole lifestyle change. I had never lived in Pakistan before; never travelled alone, and certainly never lived alone. I was becoming a man, a man whom I hoped would make my parents and grandpa-daada proud of me. A man my brother could look up to, and a man who would show my sisters the kind of man they could hope to marry one day. I needed to be the role model for my three siblings, and the local kids who looked up to me, as well as turning the heads of the kids who were on the edge of going astray.

I couldn't let my family down, or my community. The pressure to be a success in what I was embarking upon was real, most of it self-inflicted, and most of it was unnecessary pressure. So, it was time to meditate and get down on my knees and pray to Allah, surrender my anxieties to Him, as my grandpa-daada has shown me."

SIX

SURRENDERING

"As the date for my departure came ever closer, I could tell my mother's heart was overflowing with pride, fear and sorrow. She was afraid for me, and for the family, because the events of 7/7 still lingered. Her words of encouragement knew no bounds though, even in the face of disapproval from her friends who had smashed her excitement with criticisms of my parents allowing me to go 'and interfere with things back home'.

I overheard her sharing the things the aunties had been saying to her about how my trip to Pakistan would bring suspicions upon the family and the community again. Then there were the things their husbands had been saying to my father. His words of, 'What would you have him do instead?' and his never-ending patience with it all gave me the strength I needed to continue my journey. 'My love, they are only afraid that Faith will inspire changes within the families for the place they call back home, a place many have not lived in nor could live in. Remember the way they speak of the dirt, squalor, corruption, and lack of ease in Pakistan? This is all they wish to remember because it makes them feel better about their lives here in England. It helps them to feel good about never wanting to live there; and in their eyes, our son, our Faith, is giving all this ease and opportunity up to do something they themselves could never do.'

Hearing my father reassure my mother in this way, meant the world to me. He had never said anything like this to me, and probably never would say it to my face. Overhearing him say these reassuring words to my mother, confirmed for me that he knew the enormity of this trip for me. I was giving up a lot of creature comforts to go to Pakistan and teach. He knew that I was entering a whole new world that I had only seen in photos or heard about in romanticised stories of the 'homeland', when it suited, that is.

I knew my departure would be a celebration for my family, even if the local community could not comprehend why I wanted to give up such a wonderful life to live in a country where they only saw struggle, poverty, corruption and over-crowdedness, even though they would never hear anyone else say anything bad about it.

I found myself observing everything, soaking up everything around me; the flush toilet, the hidden sewerage works under the iron manhole covers, the shop fronts, appreciating the comfort of the buses, the endless supply of food and water, and of course the 24-hour connection to the internet. I was giving all of this up to go and live in a third world country I had never been to. I had not travelled outside of England, other than to Scotland and to Wales. I had noticed the differences between the three countries, and not just in the accents, but in the way of life and the depths of racism. Always with the racism. I couldn't escape it, and I found myself wondering whether I would experience prejudices in Pakistan, being British and not being able to fully understand the subtle nuances of the mannerisms and languages that only locals know.

I knew the fact that I read would have me singled out as a Brit in a heartbeat because there are very few nations on the planet that read as much as the British, or at least that is the stereotype. 'Drinking tea and reading books, oh, so terribly British!' was how Zair would mock me when I spoke of things I had learnt with Grandpa-daada and the books we shared with each other.

Going through my books, deciding which ones to take with me, I knew my closest companions would be Martin Lings and Gai Eaten, both big inspirations for me. I had read their many books over and over again and delighted in their individual journeys of setting up home in foreign lands. The way they taught and spoke about the truest essence of Islam gave me a peace in my heart, and so I knew I had to take some of them with me. Picking up copies of their books, gifted to me by Grandpa-daada, I held them up to my nose and breathed in the serenity I needed. I knew I would find more answers to my new questions within these books, as well as my Qur'aan. They all seemed to be living breathing books which always had new answers to my new questions.

Some of my questions about what to expect when I arrived in Pakistan, I had been able to find the answers to by speaking with Chacha zad and researching Islamic practices in Pakistan. I was surprised to learn that around sixty percent of Muslims in Pakistan follow Sufi saints, the main four being Pir Jalaludin, Baba Farid, Bahauddin Zakariya and Lal Shahbaz Qalandar. I knew I had to do more research on these four saints because if Sufism was about love and closeness to Allah, letting go of materialism, then surely that would mean following Allah's word, not the word of saints; as many Sunni Muslims followed the four Imams. In my logical brain, it would also mean that the dowries and honour killings were more than likely to come from the other forty percent of Muslims. As I was learning in Britain, 'othering' was a big thing, a divisive tool, one which had been used to divide Europe into 'Europe' and 'Eastern Europe'. The wealthier countries in Europe hadn't wanted to be associated with the poorer Slavic and Gypsy countries, so had othered them with the term 'Eastern Europe', something which had created a massive divide and prejudice which was as present in British society as Islamophobia and racism against Arabs and Pakistanis. The Polish, Romanians and Lithuanians had to deal with a lot of prejudice, especially in East Anglia, as you well know Moana.

And I knew I had to just let go of everything I thought I knew, and I had to surrender my logical brain, surrender to the greater plan that was laid out before me, and just listen to my intuition. I knew I wasn't always tapped into the reality of real life, because I always had my head in books, and I knew that very few Muslims understood Arabic so do not understand the teachings of the Qur'aan. I had to surrender to this knowledge and always find peace, acceptance and patience. Lots of patience. I had to become more like my Babaji, who next to Grandpa-daada, was the most patient person I knew.

One thing I was very aware of was being seen as the British Pakistani who was 'heading home to the motherland to save the savages' – as Chacha zad had so bluntly put it. And he was right, this was a danger I had to be aware of and had to pre-empt it to prevent it becoming the reality of a potential false perception. I wouldn't have the struggles many in Pakistan had, such as hunger, poverty, and a lack of education. I had the luxury of learning, thinking, and reflecting. The luxury of growing up in a country where everything worked. My stomach was full so my mind and soul could wander and understand the world, unlike many in Pakistan who were starving and struggling to survive. Getting present to all these blessings had made me see my life in a new way. I realised I had not been as grateful as I could have been.

Speaking with Mama and Babaji in one of our many private conversations, which they always made sure us kids had with them by ourselves on a regular basis, I had made Mama cry with her own gratitude. She felt my love for her and Babaji in a new way. She now saw herself in a new light, through my new observations and she became aware of just what she had given to us kids just by raising us in England, even if there was sections of the society who were bigoted, racist and Islamophobic. We knew we lived in a tolerant society, with many accepting the differences and some eager to learn about different cultures and religions. We were blessed we lived in a country where education for all was encouraged and enforced. We were blessed that we had the NHS, something so many took for granted, and abused in a variety of ways. During these conversations with our parents, Malak, Shaista, Amina and I learnt to reflect with our parents on our journey of life. Not just how far we had come, but also where we wanted to go. And even if we didn't know where we were heading in life, there was always trust, belief and encouragement. I wondered how many Pakistani children in Pakistan actually had that.

I had been blessed with a grandfather who was indeed a mystic, who believed in the possibility of attaining insight into the mysteries of transcending outside of ourself to expand on our basic and normal human knowledge. Holding the books in a firm hug against my chest with my eyes closed, I felt the direct communication with the divine, felt my intuition telling me this was the right thing to do; and although I wasn't quite in a state of spiritual ecstasy about what I was about to embark upon, I knew I was definitely someone who thoroughly enjoyed the discovery and initiations I was having into religious mysteries. And I knew that this trip was not only going to deepen my understanding of who I truly was, where my grandpa-daada had come from, and why he was so convinced in the power of the unknown galaxies within us, but it was also going to show me the truth of Pakistan, not the one portrayed in the media or the one portrayed through the different lenses of those within Bradistan.

My bags were almost packed and couldn't help but smile to myself at an analogy of the metaphysical my grandpa-daada came up with to help me understand the concept. 'Babaji, metaphysics is an idea, also known as a doctrine, or advanced reality outside of what us humans can perceive. A bit like an aeroplane once was. It was an idea that seems impossible, and a concept that many people could not comprehend. It seemed to go beyond all common sense. The thought, or perception, that this heavy object would fly through the sky taking people from one place to another, and that people would pay massive amounts of money to get on this crazy metal dart to be whizzed through the air at incredible speeds… beyond the impossible! And yet here we are, flying here, there, and everywhere.' I could see him in my mind's eye looking off into the distance, with his right hand moving through the air, just about my head, as I stood there in awe listening to him. I felt him with me, and it was this immaterial reality of feeling him with me, was how he had taught me of deep love and faith in the Divine, or as he would call it, 'Metaphysics in action.'

The older I had gotten, the more I had processed what had happened within our family with Malak and the local community after 7/7, the more I took on a more academic and philosophical view of both mysticism and metaphysics, especially when Grandpa-daada and I read about Shakespeare together, one of Martin Lings' favourite authors. Being able to share my English literature school homework with Grandpa-daada was always so fun, and rewarding, especially as I always got top marks in class for my perceptions of what Shakespeare was trying to get across.

'He is the mystic and metaphysics of literature Babaji!' Grandpa-daada would declare. 'And one of the greatest minds of his time, especially when he used the natural healing herbs to help him along.'

I hadn't quite understood what he had meant in the beginning, until of course I was old enough to understand that Shakespeare had smoked cannabis in his pipe to help him transcend to a new level of thinking – which had pleased Malak no end. 'Ah, bro! That's awesome news! So, the next time I go into school with the red eye I can simply say I was modelling the behaviour of Shakespeare! You are a legend; you do know that right?'

I wasn't quite sure the teachers, or our parents for that matter would approve, but having tried smoking weed with Malak once or twice and having been in a trance-like state after dhikr[1] practice with Grandpa-daada, I could see the similarities between the two states of consciousness. I'd also tried the whirling dance the dervishes did to bring themselves into a trance, allowing them to connect on a deeper level with Allah, which had shown me it was no different to a deep meditative state – except it was safer for me to be sat still instead of spinning around the house or out in the park. One would have resulted in trashing my parents' house, and the other would have had the local wannabe gangsters giving me grief for the rest of my time here in the area.

One of the best things about developing my practice of dhikr with Grandpa-daada was the level of patience I received from him. Sitting there with him 'trying to switch off my mind' was so frustrating because I couldn't stop the thoughts whirling around in my mind – much like the dervishes of Turkey and Persia. Pieces of knowledge kept connecting with each other, and I would see these balls of bright colourful lights with lightning flares coming off them. Sharing these visuals and connections with him would simply bring a smile to his face, and he would say, 'Welcome to the quantum realm Babaji, welcome to the quantum realm.' And then I would hear him laugh, throw his head back and tell me, 'Go on, off you go to your books and find out what the quantum realm is!'

He knew I couldn't wait to get into my books, to sit there turning page after page, grabbing another book to check the meanings and explanations, connecting even more dots in my mind – many of which had appeared to me whilst in dhikr.

Bringing the books down from my chest I looked at them again. How many of them could I realistically carry with me? Which ones could I get the best use of, and the most peace from? I was only taking a backpack with me, and 23kg is all the airlines would allow. Did I take books, or clothes? The struggle was real. In the end, I chose to take more books as I could always buy or have clothes made in Pakistan, and the books would help me to transition into my new life; and I could always use them to teach English and faith to others on my journey. And it's not like I was my sisters who would have needed 23kg just for their makeup and heels!"

---

1. **Dhikr**, (Arabic: "reminding oneself" or "mention") ritual prayer or litany practiced by Muslim mystics (Sufis) for the purpose of glorifying God and achieving spiritual perfection. Britannica, The Editors of Encyclopaedia. "dhikr". Encyclopaedia Britannica, 27 May. 2021, https://www.britannica.com/topic/dhikr. Accessed 3 December 2023.

SEVEN

BRAIN WASHED

The calls between me and Faith would last for hours. Always disappearing down rabbit holes and laughing, getting excited when we would reach the pinnacle of the conversation point. The memories of our conversations never appeared in any correct order, just randomness, like our conversations.

With the boys fast asleep, and Abdullah out of the apartment, I decided to make a spliff. My tea had gone cold, yet again, something which would have made both the boys and Faith laugh – because when did I ever drink a hot cup of tea?!

Hearing the Rizla papers as I pulled it from the packet, folding them, licking the gum, and sticking them together, right through to the gentle teasing of the tobacco out of the cigarette, and the twisting of the grinder to make the weed crumble ready to sprinkle into the Rizla on top of the tobacco was a ritual I enjoyed more than the smoking. Picking up the Rizla papers ready to roll into the perfectly made cone was something I had perfected over the twenty years of being a functioning pot head. My spliffs were admired far and wide and burned evenly all the way to the finish line. Quality ingredients deserved to be treated with respect and if I was going to smoke, then I was going to do it properly; something Faith and I agreed on.

Getting stoned together we would discuss the Endocannabinoid system[1] and CBD receptors in our bodies, how they worked, how they encouraged cancer cells to basically eat themselves, as well as how our bodies functioned better with cannabis within our bodies. Smoking wasn't the healthiest of ways to ingest it, so we would share recipes on how to make oils, butters and grind the weed so finely we could put it in our spag bol and cakes, because you know, brownies got a bit boring after a while.

We both agreed that charities such as Cancer Research were committing corporate manslaughter each day they refused to admit the healing powers of cannabis, choosing to mislead people into donating money and preying on those who were in the depths of despair and desperation.

"When will people wake up to the Big Pharma agenda and understand that they own the governments?"

This would be a question we would both ask again and again, even though we both knew that would mean people admitting they were being manipulated and lied to by doctors, charities, the government and sending their kids to a school that indoctrinated them in the worst ways to obey. Admitting there was a deception meant that they would have to question everything they knew about the world, and that took courage and an unravelling of everything, something people were not willing to do, and in most cases didn't have the capacity to do because they were so deeply programmed into the 'system' that there really was no escape.

"Some will make it out alive," he would say.

I remembered Faith telling me about the story his grandpa-daada told him about the CBD receptors in the brain and accessing the quantum realm, and a smile broke over my face, with a few more tears gently falling.

I just couldn't believe he was gone.

"Listen to me now Babaji, you know we always say, Allah knows best? Well, why do you think He created all these plants and our bodies in the way that He did? These CBD receptors we have in our magnificent bodies promote a cleaner, healthier body through the autophagy process our bodies go through, which is also increased when we fast during Ramadan. When we ingest the cannabinoids and they start to dance and whirl with the receptors in our bodies, we are cleaning out our system, a kind of real brain and body washing, if you will. When our bodies are functioning properly, then we get to sleep better, heal quickly and we can reach a higher state of consciousness. We don't just do dhikr for remembrance of Allah, we do it to connect with ourselves on a deeper level, as many non-Muslims choose to do through their meditations. When we are in, what you youngsters call a high, we can discover the Quantum Realm. Remember, Babaji, everything is designed so perfectly, and you do not need to follow a specific religion for us to connect to the Divine within ourselves."

Faith and I both knew that our connection with religion was fading fast, but our faith was getting stronger.

We both believed that to choose one religion over another one was a form of arrogance, because how could we know that we were right and everyone else was wrong? And if for every difference, there were thirty-three similarities, then surely they were all more the same than they were different.

The more we talked, the more we read, the more we shared, the more we both knew the day we would both walk away from the Islamic faith was nearer. It had to be because it just wasn't answering the questions we were asking. Looking back to history we could see how the dates of religions had been borrowed and distorted to help with invasions and the control of the people. We only had to look at the Christian missionaries and how they spread the word of the Bible, by force, by bribery, by education and by the deep layering of fear amongst the people, robbing them of the connection to the land, their ancestors and what would become known as black magic, witchcraft, and sorcery.

"You only have to look at the way in which England was taken by the Saxons, The Danes, and the Vikings. How divided it was with the different fiefdoms, and the bringing together of these different strong holds under the Church of England. The very name The Church of England tells you it is not God's word, because why would He want it to be of England, why not Scotland? Wales even! I mean, can you imagine if it was called The Church of Wales?!"

We'd both been stoned when he came out with the Church of Wales and we had laughed until we were crying, our sides ached, and we'd snorted at least a few times. We'd shared it with a few of our friends from Wales, and they puffed up their chests with one of them saying, "It would have been a tidy victory that, you know boy-o." Which made us all laugh that he'd managed to get the words 'tidy' and 'boy-o' into the sentence somehow.[2]

"One of the things that always fascinated me when Grandpa-daada would talk about the mystics, was the Witchcraft and Shamanism elements of it. You know, how they would use all the plants as salves, medicinal remedies, and the cleansing of the energetic fields. It just makes sense, because remember when the Scots invaded North America and there were those swarms of locusts and grasshoppers, and the settlers made small fires and the smoke drove the swarms away? Well, when organic farms burn tobacco leaves, or just have them growing within the greenhouses and between vines, it helps get rid of the bugs. One of the reasons we were told that crop burning was bad was because the petrochemical companies who produce the pesticides and herbicides don't make any more. And again, I just can't believe these farmers are falling for it, or even complying. Have they forgotten that the yield they would get the following year would be stronger? You know this, Moana, you're a farmer girl!"

I did know this, and it didn't matter how many things we agreed upon, it didn't matter how much passion we had for seeking out the truth, or how much we shared it with others, people were just not interested in hearing it. Much like people in power of religions were not interested in people putting faith into action. The Rabbi's, Priest's, Vicar's, Bishops, Imams were only interested in people reciting, memorising, and following orders. Never questioning why there was so much abuse, why there was so much wealth ploughed into the religious buildings rather than back into the community.

"Why can people not see what we see, Moana? Why is it so difficult for them? Why can't they see the abuses that go on within the Church, the Mosques, and the Synagogues. Take the Catholic priests in Boston back in 2002, which were raping and abusing young boys, around one thousand boys in total, and two hundred and forty-nine priests were accused of sexual abuse, which was covered up by the police, the church, government, and the press. The impact this has on the mental health of these people, and we wonder why people are leaving the church?! Then in Italy there was that famous case of Emanuela Orlandi who was abducted, abused, and killed by the priest within the Vatican! The Vatican Moana! The Pope had to be in on it because you can't get that much of a cover up without him knowing. And what about that paedophile Warren Jeffs out in the States with his Fundamental Mormon Church of the Latter-Day Saints? Multiple wives as young as twelve, all getting pregnant and being promised the Three Degrees of Glory if they had a minimum of three wives and the 'Opportunity to create worlds, galaxies, universes' putting themselves up on the same level of God by effectively making them themselves God. I mean seriously, and people think Islam is messed up with the four wives?! That Warren Jeffs guy had sixty-two children in total, and he banned all outside influences, removed literacy and numeracy, history, geography replacing all other subjects with stories of fear, damnation, and destruction. At least with Islam, the first word is clearly stated in the Qur'aan is Ikra[3], and wisdom is the second most used word in the Qur'aan after Allah. And I know it is not the religion perse, it is the lunatics which practice it, but for heaven's sake, belonging to a religion is bad for your health."

I loved it when Faith started off on one of his rants. It made a change from me going off on one. He would compare the perfect obedience women had to give to their husbands in Judaism, the various sects of Christianity and Islam, not to mention Hinduism, Sikhism, and the perfect obedience the monks in Nepal would have. Having been raised in a family where equality of the two sexes was a given, as it was stated in the Qur'aan, and practised by his family, Faith could never get his head around why women were treated as inferior, or why women felt they had to compete with men in everything men did, such as the dangerous jobs and the jobs which required the strength of men. He knew not all men were strong enough to do certain jobs, he himself included, but he did know men had a better chance of doing some jobs better than women.

One piece of logic I will never forget we came to together was the simple fact that if a woman dies, the ability for human nature to continue dies with her because she is the one who can give birth, men can't. Yes, if a man dies then his sperm dies, but men produce active sperm for much longer and produce a lot more sperm than women produce eggs. The continuation of humanity needed more women to survive than it did men. He could never understand why women belittled the job of motherhood, when it was one of the most sacred jobs known to man, if not the most sacred. It infuriated him when women would moan about having to give up their career to have children, about how it put them behind men and was an unfair advantage when it came to making money.

"How is making money more important than raising a happy, competent, and confident child who knows they are loved?! Do these women not think their child knows they are an inconvenience to their mother when they hear her moaning about their salaries? Imagine how that must make the child feel!"

Faith was all for women working and didn't have a problem with women wanting to get paid equally for the same job men did, but he hated the fact that women would say the words "just a mum" or moan about being at home with their children when they could be out working. Me running my own business was one of the things he admired about me.

"You know, one thing I heard you say in one of your interviews that made me respect you so much was that running your own business was a form of female activism because no one was going to tell you whether you could or could not take time off to be with your children or watch them sing in the school play with a tea towel on their head. Women can earn whatever they want, and they do not need to settle. They have the choice to ask for more money, make more money and be as free as they want, but they don't ask for it, and they don't go after what they say they want, and yet they say Muslim women are oppressed. They too are oppressed, but not by the hijab they think Muslim women are oppressed by, but their own lack of self-belief. As you Brits like to call it, pot calling the kettle black."

The fact that he had heard that interview surprised me, and I actually asked him if he had been stalking me. His response made me laugh because he replied with, "Not long enough!"

I hadn't heard of the paedophile Warren Jeffs, and so spent time researching it. What I learned disgusted me and saw much of the abuse was directed at the men as it was the women. Not in the same ways of course, but the fact that the men had to work as slaves giving all their business income to 'the Prophet' so they could build the 'Church of Zion', and the young boys were slaves working for free because of their 'devotion' to the Prophet himself Warren Jeffs, made my Mama heart break. If Jeffs, or the bishop of the community, Fred Jessop, aka 'Uncle Fred', wanted a new wife, he just claimed up, ending up with twenty wives. Everyone within this cult, which is effectively what it was, lost their homes and businesses to Warren Jeffs, who also controlled the police, fire brigade, and the curriculum taught in the classrooms, which were also held within the congregational hall. What astounded me the most was that Warren Jeffs, and his Church of Zion went on to become number one *human trafficking organisations in the US with the young girls being the property of the church.*

It infuriated Faith that Islam was shamed and demonised when Islam stopped slavery of all kinds and held women on an incredibly elevated level, especially mothers. I could tell he was really struggling with everything he was discovering about religions around the world, and the way he would then look at the way in which Islam was portrayed, especially in Britain.

The media was full of stories of young girls being

married young, not educated, being labelled as immigrants and drug dealers. Muslims were being targeted for all the evil that was happening in the world, and things were getting scary for both our families. With many refugees escaping wars in other countries, with Islam being used as the go-to excuse, instead of it being the real reasons of control of the land and resources, there was a lot of anti-Arab, anti-Pakistani and anti-Muslim hate bubbling up. In fact, there was a lot of anti-foreigner feelings rising up everywhere. A German friend of ours had her car damaged with anti-foreigner messaging because it had a German license plate. Many of the news stories tried to focus on the fact that women and girls were in danger because they had no education, no English skills, and were being forced into marriages against their will. Arranged marriages were just an alien concept to modern day Britain, well apart from within the upper echelons of society such as the monarchy who were still marrying for country alliances and keeping property within families. But that was okay, they were white Europeans and British, so that was allowed. Not so much if you were brown and chose to wear a hijab, though.

The more Faith saw of what was going on, the more he was being driven to leave England, he just didn't want to be around the bigotry and stupidity that was going on. "Can't people see the human rights violations that are happening left, right and centre in places such as Afghanistan with the Taliban are no different to the ones happening on US soil? How is it the police forces and governments can get away with doing nothing, whilst sex crimes and forced marriages are taking place, and the women and children are made to wear clothing from decades ago? Isn't this the same thing happening to the women and girls of Afghanistan? They speak of respecting the religious beliefs of US fundamentals, but demonise the Taliban? Both are wrong in my opinion, especially with the four hundred and thirty-seven children in the custody battle between Jeffs and the US government, which I think is, or was, the US's largest custody battle on record. But why is it white folk are allowed religious freedom, but brown folk are not? And where do we draw the line between religious freedom and morality? Something needs to be done Moana, and I feel hopeless just sitting here in England doing nothing when I could be doing something back in Pakistan, or even Afghanistan."

When he mentioned his desire to go to Pakistan or Afghanistan, I knew he had been thinking about it for a long time. I told him he was like my mum in that respect because she would only tell me she was ill if she was really ill. She only had a cold when in fact she needed antibiotics or God forbid had had a heart attack – which to this day, thank goodness she hadn't had.

He no longer felt safe in England, which saddened me, but I understood why. I would often look at Salah and Marai and wonder what life had in store for them being Arabs in England. Would they be subjected to bullying, attacks and the deeply embedded racism and prejudices. England was home to many bigots, the English Defence League and Britain First, or racist thugs for want of a better term. The political arm of both those groups was UKIP, the United Kingdom Independence Party, not that the United Kingdom was united, nor a Kingdom – but with the health of the Queen not looking so great, that would soon change. Faith, many of our friends and me believed that wanting independence from the rest of Europe was a bad idea, but with the spin the politicians were putting on things, especially hammering home the anti-Muslim, anti-immigration messages, and with the amount of people who were so blind to see the greatness that the diversity in England brought to the country, it was going to be a close call when the referendum eventually happened, because it would happen, for that we were all certain – when the politicians got their acts together, that is.

The anti-Muslim feeling across England led to many people across the country in all walks of life speaking out about why they no longer followed religion, and some of them made some bloody good arguments for it, many that mirrored our own; but it wasn't about losing our faith, just the man-made constructs that had been added to the faith to control the people throughout the ages.

"It's funny you know Moana, your parents don't believe in God or religion because it causes too many wars, and my parents have a deep faith with the structure of the Islamic religion, but even they are questioning whether there would be peace without religion and if everyone just had faith in themselves, each other, and the planet. They were even talking last night about all these terror attacks going on, and how these tribal and angry Muslims from the mountains are causing problems for everyone else, thinking that their way, with their limited education, and lack of knowledge about the world, is the way everyone should live. It's like the arrogance of the Americans thinking they know what is best for everyone, when only 45% of the US civilian population have passports, and around 10% of those are in the military. How can they know anything about the rest of the world, when they are so self-absorbed and insular? Most of them only travel to Canada and Mexico anyway, and before 9/11 they didn't need a passport to travel to either."

Hearing the point he was making, I had to add, "I don't think we can say that they only go to Canada and Mexico, I mean there is Israel and Cuba, don't forget. And now there are quite a number of the younger generation coming here to England because they 'love our accent'. Oh, and don't forget France for the romance and Amsterdam for the drugs and prostitutes – if we are going to stereotype to the fullest." Just to reign him in and show how our own prejudicial stereotypes about the Americans had us lumping all US citizens into one pot, like they lumped all Muslims – or rather the Moslems – into one. "I really fucking hate the way they say Muslims. I mean, can they not read?! Just like they say A-Rab rather than Arab, or I-rak instead of Iraq. Grrr!"

Faith was in fits of laughter. "Oh my god, listen to the teacher come out in you! You are so going to be a great English teacher one day. You should teach English when you go to Egypt, you know. You'll be able to teach there, unlike here where teachers are more administrators rather than teachers. Man, I'd hate to be a teacher in this country. I am so glad I am joining Teachers Without Borders."

Remembering this conversation with him, I smiled because I had become a teacher here in Egypt, and I was loving it! We had both discussed me becoming a teacher and how it had always been a dream of mine when I was younger, but there was no way I could teach the way I wanted to if I had been in England. That didn't mean there wasn't a conflict with the Heads of Department here in Egypt, because there was, loads of them. My dream of becoming a teacher also meant I got to train and coach my teaching assistant, Ms Amira to become a teacher. She would help me with some of the lesson plans and marking – as well as navigate the political situation the Uprising has presented us all with. The amount of knowledge, training and experience I was giving her had gotten me into a lot of trouble, mainly with the other teachers as they were not training their teaching assistants to become teachers, just treating them like servants, which was something I never understood.

Living in Egypt and teaching in the schools made it even clearer to me that it didn't matter where in the world any of us lived, there was terror everywhere, and it didn't always come from overseas or by the military and governments either. It could happen, and was happening within the very schools we taught in.

---

1. https://norml.org/marijuana/library/recent-medical-marijuana-research/introduction-to-the-endocannabinoid-system
2. The word 'tidy' is a well-known word used by many Welsh people, much like the English like to use the word 'proper' to describe something well made, well done or substantial. And the word 'boy-o' is term of endearment most Welsh use at the end of their sentences when addressing males.
3. Ikra = read

EIGHT

TERRORISM

"I just cannot comprehend what is going on in the world, Moana. People say they want peace, but then they hate on others from a different country, different religion, language and even gender. How can people be so hateful to one another, and all this abuse in the world? I mean I know it is all engineered this way, but another shooting in a US school by a student?! What is wrong with these people? They are fucking up their kids so much, the kids are going around shooting other kids!"

I had never seen Faith so angry before, or so traumatised by events he saw on the news, not even when the 7/7 bombing happened. Not even when he and his family had their home raided, and his brother arrested, along with many other Pakistani families across the country. He especially hated it when kids got hurt, abused, or killed. These events always impacted him deeply.

"They're just kids Moana! How do these kids get to have that much hatred in them that they want to kill other kids?" And that was the moment he broke. Seeing him cry, shoulders moving up and down, rocking back and forth, I had never seen a grown man cry so much. I knew this was a much deeper release of the build-up of trauma he and his family had gone through. I was taken aback by it and did what the British do best in times like these and put the kettle on to make a cup of tea. He needed space and time alone to cry it out, and making tea was more about giving him that space rather than the drinking of tea.

"Here, drink this." I said, handing him the mug of tea, black and sugar free, just the way I like it.

"What is this? This is not tea! Where's the milk and sugar? And the chai?" He teased with tears still falling.

"Think you need to think about a tissue for your nose Dude, more than the milk, sugar and chai," I responded nodding to the tissues on the coffee table.

With the tea sorted, and his nose, I sat and listened to him offload everything that had built up within him.

"I just don't get how the US demonises Islam whilst sheltering the Christian corruption and abuses only to take notice when something like the WACO Massacre happens, with that fruit loop David Koresh, you know, the founder and cult leader of The Davidians. You know it was him and that massacre which led to Timothy McVeigh, that Gulf War Veteran, bombing Oklahoma on the second anniversary of the WACO massacre? He watched it on the TV live, and the police, the military and the government all knew that McVeigh had long espoused anti-government and white supremacist views. It was one of the reasons he was rejected by the Green Berets during his U.S. Military Service. And I don't get how when it is a white Christian who bombs a marathon, or goes on a shoot-out in a school, his faith is never mentioned. It's never Christian bombs/shootings/massacres is it? No! But the moment a Muslim does something the first word in the headline is Muslim. The double standards make me, how do you say it? Two cups of tea cross? Well, I am at about four cups of tea cross, Moana!"

He took breath and poured himself some more tea from my favourite blue teapot, big enough for his four cups of tea and my two.

"There are just so many double standards. And why is it when the US go on a rampage in someone else's country, terrorising the life out of the locals, telling them that they cannot live, believe or worship the way they want to, that is not terrorism? How is turning up in someone else's country in tanks, walking their streets with semi-automatics and shooting things up, how is that not terrorism? What right do they have in doing that? Just because the kinship systems are different. Or the culture is different? They did it to the Native Americans when they first colonised the lands of North America and they think they can still keep doing it the world over. And those kids Moana, what did they ever do to deserve being shot to death and now being afraid to go to school, to learn, to make a real difference in the world? How can they learn in such conditions now? And what has it done to their sense of safety? So many hopes and dreams shattered in one afternoon by a looney tune who is so damaged by what they themselves have been through and indoctrinated with that they saw no other option than to shoot everyone else. Those poor kids Moana."

At which point the tears started falling again, so I just

let him cry it out. He sat back with his back against the couch and his head resting backwards. He was trying to regain his composure with his breathwork techniques, and in between breaths the words, "Those poor kids, what did they do to deserve a world like this?"

Eventually, he fell asleep on the couch, so I put a blanket over him and went into the kitchen to start on dinner. He'd be hungry when he woke up after all that crying, and I knew he'd be happy to have my roast potatoes and homemade cheeseburgers. Just as I had finished putting everything in the oven to cook, I saw the boys coming in through the fence at the top of the garden with armfuls of sticks each for the firepit. I went outside to meet them and told them to be quiet if they went inside as Uncle was sleeping on the couch. Neither of them went inside as they had more sticks to go collect from the woods. They raced each other back to the top of the garden, and as brother's tended to do, they competed over who was strong enough to carry the bigger logs they'd also found. I laughed when they both came back with arms full of logs that would keep the fire burning for a few hours. "Where on earth did you get those?" I asked.

"From the woods. The wind has blown down loads of trees so there are loads of these."

"Is that why you are both really dirty?"

"Yep! And you do always say that if we come back in clean, we've not had enough fun." Salah reminded me in his cheeky way.

"Yes, I do say that. Well, don't bother changing because you still need to finish building the fire for when dinner is ready, which it should be in about fifteen minutes."

"What have we got for dinner? Do we have the cheeseburgers and roast potatoes like you promised?" Marai pleaded.

"Yes, we do, and I am about to go back in and make the salad. Oh, and whilst I remember. Uncle is upset about the school shooting that happened yesterday in the US, so just be mindful of that, okay?"

"Okay, Americans, why are they always shooting people? They should just get rid of the guns," responded Salah.

"They can't Salah. It's their second agreement in their constipation, no, not their constipation, I mean… their … what is it called Mama?" giggled Marai.

Salah and I were too busy laughing at the word constipation to even begin to tell him the word he was looking for was constitution. And it was these moments that I enjoyed the most with the boys. Their knowledge of so many things and the uncomplicated way they looked at life, and the mistakes in the verbiage they used.

Either the laughing or the natural end of Faith's nap had ended, and he joined us up on the patio area. "What are you all laughing at?"

"Marai just said Americans were constipated," giggled Salah, making us all laugh even more.

"No, I didn't," giggled Marai.

"I need to go in and make the salad. You boys get the fire sorted and bring the plates and cutlery outside and lay the table. We'll eat out here tonight," I said, as I made my way down the steps to the back door and back into the kitchen.

With the kitchen window slightly open, I could hear the three of them discussing the US Constitution together and why guns were a bad idea. Faith was sharing with them more of his knowledge, the natural teacher that he was. "It doesn't matter how much we didn't understand someone's way of life, we should do our best to try and understand it, what impact the age of the country was, the landscape and the climate. Sometimes boys, the terrain of a country makes it difficult for those who live there to travel or to go from one community to the next. And sometimes the lack of resources and exposure to the rest of the world means some communities are living in what some would call the past. And it is these differences in understanding time which impacts the way in which we all evolve."

"And how much food people have, because if they are hungry we can't learn," chirped in Marai.

"That's right Marai. If people are more concerned about eating, staying warm and staying alive, as well as keeping the family surviving for generations, then other things won't matter to them," continued Faith. "That's why we always have to think of seven reasons why someone does something, or behaves in a certain way, and if…"

"… if we can think of seven things, we have to think of seven more, and just keep going…" said the boys in chorus.

"Akla gaahiz!"[1] I call through the window, and they all come running down the stairs to wash their hands in the kitchen sink.

"Where's dinner?" asked Salah.

"I didn't think you would be that quick to come down. The plates are just warming. Is the table set yet? It doesn't look like it. Here, take the water, glasses, and the cutlery," I said, handing everything to the boys. "And you can take the buns, cheese, salad and pickles for the burgers Faith."

"They smell so good Moana!" Faith said as he walked back outside, only just managing to dodge out of the way as the boys came running back in to get the burgers and roast potatoes.

As we sat eating, Marai was quiet. "What are you thinking Marai?" asked Faith.

"I am thinking about how angry and upset that person was who shot all those children. And how sad and confused his mum and dad must be that he did it because I know I get angry with Salah when he plays with my things, but I couldn't shoot him, or any of the children at school."

"You're right, he must have been really angry and upset, and so must his parents be, and maybe no one will ever know why he did it. His parents will also be feeling very scared and alone right now as well as confused and upset, I can imagine," I replied.

"Why will they be angry and scared?" asked Salah.

"Because the other parents will now probably hate them," answered Marai.

"Oh." Salah paused before adding, "These burgers are great Mum, thank you!"

"You're welcome Baaba and thank you for saying you are enjoying them," I said with a grateful heart, not just because of the compliment, but because the boys were contemplating what had happened and felt free to discuss it.

"I think we should say what we are happy for. I'll go first," declared Marai. "I am happy England doesn't have guns. And for these delicious and juicy cheeseburgers, but not the pickles."

"But not the pickles," laughed Salah, adding, "And I am grateful for the woods because we get to play and pick up sticks for our fire pit."

After dinner, and the fire, the boys went up to shower and get ready for their bedtime story, Faith washed up, came upstairs, and thanked us all for an enjoyable day. He was heading home as he still had things to sort out for his new teaching job with Teachers Without Borders.

He had a lot to think about, especially as he could have his location changed at a moment's notice, depending on where TWB needed him to go. He also needed some proper sleep. The boys and I hugged him goodbye, and he left. The boys had chosen *The Enormous Crocodile* by Roald Dahl.

"Mama?"

"Yes, Salah."

"You know what we were talking about earlier, the shooting in that school, and it being terrorism, well… the crocodile is also a terrorist isn't he? Because he is scaring all the animals."

I looked at Salah and smiled, "Yes, Baaba, you could say that. But being afraid isn't quite as bad as being terrified. There is quite a bit of difference. Such as, I am scared of needles, but not terrified of them."

"What terrifies you then?" asked Marai.

"To be honest Baaba, nothing at the moment, and for that I am grateful. Quite a few things scare me, like losing you both… actually, I tell you what does terrify me?" I said looking at Salah with a smile on my face. "When you, Mister! hide from me in the clothes when we go shopping and I think someone has stolen you. THAT terrifies me. The thought that someone may have stolen you."

"But … I am just playing Hide and Seek Mama," Salah replied.

"I know you are Baaba, and I love playing Hide and Seek with you, but we have to make sure everyone knows we are playing it and have to play it in a place where there aren't so many strangers around. Okay?"

"Okay."

"Do you have any more questions Baaba?" I asked.

"No, so you can finish the story now," he instructed.

"Yes, boss."

"Hear that Marai," teased Salah, "I'm the boss!"

"That's what you think. Now be quiet so Mama can finish the story."

"Okay," replied Salah.

"See, told you you're not the boss," laughed Marai.

---

1. 'Akla gaahiz' means 'food is ready'.

NINE

NEVER QUESTION

The memories that were flooding back to me as I remembered the conversations with Faith over the few short years we knew each other, and had taken for granted, were adding to the tears that were falling; but they were also adding to the depths of gratitude that I was feeling for having met him. When he opened up to me about the home invasion, and how the terror attacks had truly impacted his family and community, my own experiences of being spat on, losing friends and business contracts just because I was married to an Arab, paled into insignificance.

With Abdullah working away, and not being around much to have mental gymnastics with, Faith had been a great close second to a mental sparring partner. The depths of the mind we would explore, the concepts and ideas we would delve into allowed us to ask deeper questions, encouraged us both to read more books and research the various different topics, such as scientific exploration of the energetic fields, the human body and those who were leading figures within Sufism, such as the Sufi Master Al Ghazali.

The more we both philosophised about life and it's meaning the more we both started to lean into the teachings and way of life of Sufism. Yes, we both enjoyed the theoretical science of religion, but we both knew the deeper faith which all religions spoke of, meant the content which was studied from books or learnt from a master, had to be activated in life. Everything had to be put into practice, rather than just recited and memorised. The teachings were a lifestyle choice, a balance and harmony with nature, and the way we conducted ourselves in society. Taking guidance from the Sufi masters and reconciling them with today's modern world, Faith found it easier to withdraw from the masses so he could find seclusion to reflect and consider who he was, why he was here and what his purpose was.

He claimed that leaning more into Sufism was helping him become closer to his grandpa-daada, and the more we discussed, the more we tested theories together, the deeper our forgiveness, and our faith in a higher power, entity and energy force. Without both forgiveness and faith, we would have both become bitter, angry and heavens only knows where our journey would have led us. The Islamic practice of 'think of seven reasons why someone does something, then think of another seven, and keep going, was a game changer in empathy and forgiveness. We both knew the things we were learning were taking us further away from organised religion, because the more religions we studied the more we realised they were *all* teaching us the fundamental basics of humanity. How could we follow just one? How could we say that any of the individual religions were right, and the others were wrong? That would just be arrogant and righteous, something neither of us wanted to be. The life of a nomad was a natural way of humanity in the beginning of times, which Al-Ghazali referred to as itinerancy, and it underpinned much of the Sufi lifestyle and teachings, because how could we learn to love, if we didn't know what love meant in the wider scope of humanity?

One of the biggest challenges we both had with religion is that religious leaders never seemed positive about encouraging the followers of the religion to question it or dive deeper into other religions. The three main religions of Judaism, Christianity and Islam were all Abrahamic faiths, so why were they not studied together? Ego pretty much answered that question. Along with fear of letting go and surrendering to a new truth, to an evolution of self and to losing money.

"Everyone is just following, and yet they never stop to ask how scholars of the religions ever got to the point of understanding that they did. How can you become a scholar if you don't question what you are studying?" Faith would ask this question in pretty much every debate he ever had with people on the subject of religion.

Our conversations around questioning the subject of questioning would run pretty true to the theory that if we never question religion, our faith or ourselves, how can we grow in knowledge and humanity? To keep reading things which confirm our faith actually weakens it because it is not tested. It is like any scientific hypothesis, thesis, or idea, it needs to be tested for its strength. Imagine building something as simple as a chair and not testing it! We would only find out it was no good when it was challenged with weight and movement, so surely the most logical perspective is to read other holy texts, ideas on faith and science, history, economics, and physics, because it is going to be an important thing. It gives everything context and tests everything! If we genuinely believe, and believe with wisdom, then our faith will hold up. But if it is based on blind following of what others tell us, and reading a translation of another language, then how can we have deep faith? The truth is we can't, and to be honest, how is blind faith any different to grooming someone? The truth is it isn't.

Grooming is simply building a relationship with someone, playing on their fears to build trust with them, and getting them to do whatever we want them to, just like so many parents and the religious leaders do when it comes to blind faith. How can we trust something we haven't had the opportunity to explore and question without fear? We speak of religious freedoms, but where is the freedom to question everything we are taught and told about religion? We are told not to mix with gentiles, heretics, infidels, and every other name given to non-believers of a particular faith we have been taught to follow by our parents or society, but why shouldn't we? If we honestly believe the All-knowing Almighty created us all and the earth, and then scattered us upon this vast planet we inhabit far and wide to live different lives in vastly different landscapes and climates, then surely he did it for a reason, other than to fight? If we believe this All-Knowing Almighty entity is All-Wise, and each faith teaches us to love and be kind, to learn, to read and be educated and be the very best version of self, then surely this in and of itself tells us to get to know and learn from each other, rather than hate, condemn and destroy. That just didn't make sense to either of us.

The biggest difference Faith had to the majority of the Pakistani community he came from was that he had a very different view on finances and money. He believed, like I did, that the more money we had, the more greatness we could achieve for ourselves and others.

"This financial piety aspect, where to have money is to not be humble, how ridiculous is that – and a contradiction! They collect money after every service, regardless of the religion and place of worship – to maintain the building, for the community etc, but where is that money really going? And surely if we have to donate to charity to purify our earnings and our souls, the more money we make, the more we donate and the more purified we are. And this Christian belief thing about purification, original sin, and babies being born in sin – what the hell is all that about? How is a newborn baby born in sin? The poor thing has just been born and was made during the time of intimacy between the parents! I know not every birth comes from the most amazing orgasm, and some women are raped, but how is that the unborn child's fault? How is that going to make the baby sinful? And if the Christians were allowed to question this, and they read their holy book properly, they would know in the Ezekiel 18:4, 20, chapter it clearly says that sin is something we do, and the child does not inherit from their parents."

"I often wonder if it comes from the generational wounding in some way, because remember we inherit these wounds through genetic mutations, the epigenetics theory, which when we do the inner work, we can actually alter to a new genetic signature." I answered one day after having spent months researching generational wounding, genomes, and epigenetics.

"Yeah, I get that, and I need to explore epigenetics a bit more – thank you for reminding me of it. It is still not being born from sin though and deserve punishment – which brings me onto abortion. I don't know how I stand on this, especially when it comes to rape, Moana."

"That is a difficult subject because I don't know how I would feel if I got pregnant after being raped. To know that the child growing within me is the child of someone who raped me, having to look at the child every day knowing the act that conceived them. That is a hard one to have a take on. Yes, it is not the child's fault that they were conceived, and yes, everything happens for a reason, but honestly, I don't think I could carry a pregnancy after rape and then raise the child."

"What about if you had a really dangerous, life threatening dis-ease you were carrying, that showed up on the scans and blood tests, would you abort the baby then?"

"Again, it would depend on the type of life threatening dis-ease we are talking about. If we mean, life threatening in the sense that the child wouldn't be able to walk, talk or hear, more of a restrictive impact on life, rather than imminent death, then probably. It is all subjective. I didn't want to know about any illnesses or dis-eases the boys might have, because I would face whatever came my way and trust the process. There's learning in it all for all of us. If the child dies in infancy, then without them becoming a lab rat for research purposes then, yes, I will go ahead with the pregnancy, because what if the doctors are wrong? What if they misdiagnose? Should Stephen Hawking have been aborted because of the disabilities? In many cultures, the answer would have been yes, but thank goodness he wasn't. If he hadn't been born in England to educated and activist parents, then maybe he wouldn't have been blessed with the opportunities he was. They weren't rich, but they used their talents and networks to give him the best opportunities they could. Had he been born in Egypt he would have probably been set on the side of the road selling tissues. If he had been born in China, then there would have been a huge social stigma around his birth and would have been believed to be a bad on from past sins of the parents – which ties in with the Christian belief of original sin and being born of sin. Everything is relative – which is probably what sparked in Stephen Hawking's brain on some level of consciousness given he studied relativity."

Remembering his touché and laugh when I came out with this last bit brought a smile to my face. I looked at my watch and realised that Abdullah was still not home. Having been crying so much and finished the joint I was now hungry, or rather had the munchies, so I got up to go to the kitchen to make some brownies. Abdullah was going to make them the next day anyway, so I decided to make them whilst I waited for him to get home, which could be anytime given the events happening in Egypt at the moment. Would he get caught up in the crossfire of the military against the people, or get kidnapped as a foreign spy? Thinking of the conversation with the boys about what is terrorism, and looking at events unfolding here in Egypt, the fear of not knowing whether our loved ones coming back, or if our home was going to get raided because of his work as a fixer for the BBC, and my blogging and interviews with the BBC, I had to ask myself if I was living with terror, because it didn't feel like it. I felt numb. I wasn't surprised and had accepted the situation as it was.

Had facing my own mortality before this with Salah's birth numbed me to death so there wasn't any terror left in me?

Had Faith done so much research into the concept and constructs of religion, the sexual, domestic, financial, and spiritual abuses, not forgetting the control of the masses, had numbed him to the fact that he could be stoned to death back in Pakistan for walking away from Islam?

Questions we had both explored repeatedly consisted of wondering when did terror actually kick in? And how many of the terrors of the world were actually terrors, rather than just fear of the unknown – created by mass media? We'd debated about whether the word terror was just a media hyped and overused word now, so much so that humanity had expanded its comfort zone to accept more fear, so terror didn't appear as a big deal anymore? And if people actually stopped watching the news and believing the media, would the fear of terror itself go away?

When we saw the media reporting on the 'War on Terror' we'd discussed whether the terror inflicted on those in the Middle East and Southeast Asia by the white Western world more acceptable than on the terror attacks by suicide bombers simply because the media said so in a way that fuelled racial hatred and Islamophobia?

One of the hardest areas of exploration for us both was whether the terror experienced by the young children who were sexually abused by the religious leaders trusted to take care of them non-existent due to the subtle grooming that had taken place, until later in life?

When I'd asked him about what he would do if he saw a woman getting stoned to death in Pakistan for bringing shame on the family by refusing to marry the man chosen for them by other family members, or because they had sexual intercourse prior to marriage, he'd replied with, "Why was stoning only referenced to classical Islamic jurisprudence, also known as Fiqh, as a form of Sharia Law on the basis of hadith[1] when in fact stoning was not mentioned in the Qur'aan but was mentioned in the Torah and the Talmud? No one ever mentions the Jews when it comes to stoning the women, only Muslims, and isn't diverting the fear away from one religion onto another a form of passive aggressive terrorism?"

Faith had gone so far down the rabbit hole, or rather the worm hole, that all these questions had led him to an unravelling within himself, leaving him with many dark nights of the soul. "Why is it Moana, when we seek more clarity on these issues, all we do is end up with more questions, and when we seek inner peace and wish to help others generate the confidence within themselves to ask the important questions, we are the ones who end up suffering more?"

I didn't have the answer for him, all I could do was be the sounding board and safety net for him to fall into when he needed it. He may not have been my blood brother, but he was a brother to me in so many ways. I just wish we had more time together before he'd left for Pakistan, and I'd left for Egypt.

And now, hearing of his death, reflecting on the conversations and memories we'd created, I wondered whether he had found his inner peace before his death.

---

1. Assumed sayings and actions attributed to the Islamic prophet Muhammad

TEN

HOME INVASION

The number of home invasions happening across Egypt, especially in Cairo and Alexandria, was increasing, and each time they had happened, I thought back to how so many of my friends back in England had been interrogated following 9/11 and 7/7 – just because they were Pakistani and had either been to Pakistan recently, or they'd had a friend or relative come to visit.

It seemed that there was no rhyme or reason, and when Faith told me about the fear and isolation he and his family had been through following the 7/7 bombings, I listened, hard.

"It was awful, Moana. We are British, and it is our capital city that has been bombed. It was individuals who had executed this terror attack apparently in our name, but they had nothing to do with us, or our beliefs. We were as concerned, if not more so, than the rest of England, because it wasn't just that our country had been the target of a terror attack, but us too because we are also Muslims. We share the same colour skin, the same religion – even though the faith is very different – and we are already being seen and targeted as terrorists, even before Isha prayer! By people in our own neighbourhoods who had known us all our lives.

Seeing our non-Pakistani neighbours avoid eye contact, refuse to speak with us, or allow their children to play with the Pakistani kids in schools – not forgetting the outsiders coming to Bradford just to insult and attack us, blaming us for the bombings – was painful and incomprehensible. These were people who we had shared countless meals and conversations with, neighbours who had been looking out for each other day in and day out for decades, and here we now were, enemies, just because some lunatics decided to blow up the underground.

But that night, when the banging and shouting happened in the early hours of the morning, police barging into our home and ransacking the place, putting Malak in handcuffs and leading him out the door, with Babaji demanding to know what was going on and pushed aside by the police, Mama crying and becoming hysterical, and my sisters trying to calm them both – and I just stood there, frozen like an idiot. I'll never forget the way Malak looked at me and told me to take care of everyone. He knew this wasn't going to be easy on our family, he knew that the neighbours would talk, as they often did about things they did not know. That looked snapped me out of the fear I was feeling and I felt the presence of grandpa-daada, and as I did I turned towards Babaji and told him I would deal with this, that everything would be okay. He needed me to the be firstborn son, to step up and take care of this because he was too angry, too unaware of how things worked in society these days – even though he was still one of the smartest of men that I knew. As I stepped out of the front door, I saw so many police riot vans, and Malak, our friends and uncles being put in the back of police cars, prison security vans. It seemed as if the whole neighbourhood was under suspicion. And then I saw our local Imam being escorted with his head held high and looking serene and peaceful, almost in defiance and, as always, in his gentle pious manner. Even in our heated disagreements he had always remained gentle, feisty, and passionate, but always gentle.

With so many homes raided, and the scale of this sting operation, you can imagine the number of hysterical women and angry men out in the street. Everyone wanted to know why our brothers, sons, and uncles – and a few of the women – were being taken away. Where were they being taken? What had the police learnt that none of us knew about the people we had lived with for years? Were other Pakistani communities also being raided? And why so many? Was it the chicken feed strategy of throwing as many seeds as possible to the ground and seeing which ones get pecked up? I turned around and went back in the house to find Mama sitting in grandpa-daada's chair, with my sisters either side of her, with Babaji in the kitchen making chai. A scene that made me smile to myself in the chaos because in the most English of Pakistani ways, tea was being made to make the situation better, and I wondered how many English people actually realised that the Pakistani's made as much tea as the English in times of distress.

'What, did you see my boy? What is going on?' asked Babaji and Mama in unison.

'They are taking almost thirty in total, mostly men and about seven women from what I can see, from this street, the next and the next. All ages, and they are taking the Imam Haji Ahkbar with them,' I replied. Not that this surprised me in the least.

'Walaah! Astagfirullah! The Imam?!' chorused my parents and sister, which surprised me, because why did they think that both Malak and I had stopped going to mosque, and Grandpa-daada had preferred us to be taught about Islam at home. Babaji had only allowed himself to see the good in everyone, made excuses for Imam Haji Ahkbar, 'he's just stuck in his ways'. And now this.

'Yes, the Imam. And going by what the media has been saying, it would appear that the police think the *undisclosed mosque* is our local mosque. Things are going to get crazier than ever around here from now on, you do know that, don't you? Everything we have ever done, everything we have ever said, and every place, lecture, connection we have ever had with anyone is now going to be scrutinised, twisted, and used against us all; especially as Malak has been taken.'

'Why Malak though? He is the least religious out of all of us!' sobbed Amina. 'He never goes to mosque. He stays home or goes to his friends to smoke pot. He is the least likely person amongst us all, except you of course Mama, to do anything radical!' She was starting to tip over from emotional to angry, and I had seen her get like this only once or twice before.

'Amina is right!' added Shaista, 'Out of all of us he is the least religious, hasn't prayed for ages, and nor would he hurt a fly. He is a pot head for heaven's sake, all he wants to do is get stoned, eat pakoras and finish off all the halawa! This is insanity. Come on, we're going to the police station to sort this out. Amina, you stay here and look after Mama and Babaji, Faith and I are going to sort this out and get Malak back home.'

She grabbed me by the arm, grabbed our coats and told me she was driving, which in her heightened state, I wasn't sure was the best course of action, but knowing how she was a much more confident driver than I was, even though I passed my driving test a year before her, I didn't want to argue. Plus, Shaista was not the kind of woman you would want to argue with.

'When we get to the police station, what's the plan?' She asked.

'Hey? You were the one who dragged me out of the house in the middle of the night, thinking that we were even going to be allowed in the police station. How do you know they are not going to throw us into a police cell?' I questioned her.

Her silence told me that she had not thought that far ahead in advance, which was typical of her really, but she always managed to pull everything out of the bag and come up smelling of roses – to use two very English phrases. The car was silent for the next few minutes, and then I heard her take a breath which told me that my little sister was swallowing down her tears. 'Let them fall before we go in. Don't let them see weakness in you Shaista. Let it out now. In fact, pull over for a minute or two and do your thing.' I told her.

'Do my thing? Do my thing? Our brother and half the men we know in our neighbourhood have just been arrested on suspicion of being those bloody lunatics who blew up London, and you want me to *do my thing*?! I mean Malak, of all people! Our own brother! And you, you are so bloody calm about it all! And Babaji, after his initial anger, making bloody chai!' Tears were now streaming down her face and her hands were shaking, then her shoulders started moving up and down as the fear, tiredness and shock started moving through her body. Then I heard a noise coming from her I had never heard before. A wailing I had only heard coming from old women in old movies, a raw guttural sound that came from the depths of her soul. My baby sister was in pain, and I could do nothing to ease it.

And just then, my phone rang. 'Babaji?'

'Yes, my boy. Where are you now? How is your sister?' my father asked, as if he had heard the noise that had just come out of her from miles away.

'We have about ten minutes before we get there, but we needed to pull over for a moment to compose ourselves and figure out what we were going to do and say when we get there,' I told him.

'Okay, and Shaista, she is okay? You know how hot headed she is. I am glad you are with her, my son. You are the light we need in these moments of darkness. Your grandpa-daada will be proud of you.'

Hearing my father say these words to me, moved me

deeply. He knew I was feeling grandpa-daada and the serenity he always brought to our family, and amongst all the stress and fear, I too felt tears burn my eyes and fall. 'He is with us Babaji, always is. We are only going to ask if they need our help, to find out why they have taken Malak, and we are going to bring him home with us.'

'Your certainty is strong my son. Your mother will need to hear this for herself. Here she is.' I heard him pass the phone to my mother with the words 'here you are my love', both speaking more now in English than I had ever heard them do. Was the fact that these arrests, due to us being Pakistani, were required for us all to shift from my parents' mother tongue to English? Was this what was needed for them to protect themselves and us from being guilty by association, and to prove we were law abiding English people? A leap away from us being associated from the London Bombers?

'Where are you Babaji? How is your sister? I know you are holding us all together, but your sister, she needs you to be her calming force. Please keep her safe from her own mouth. You know how she can run away with herself in the moment of heat in situations. I am trusting you, my boy, to be the man you were born to be, for her, for your brother, our dear sweet Malak...' and at that her voice trembled and her grief overtook her.

Because it was a grief. A grief of everything she had come to believe England stood for: fairness, security, a feeling of safety, and of course the grief for her youngest son being now tainted forever more with the stigma of being arrested for terrorism – even if he was innocent, which, of course, we knew he was. The unravelling of our community had only just begun, and the accusations, the fear in people's eyes, the distrust of every Pakistani in the eyes of others was now about to change our lives in ways none of us could really comprehend. We'd seen and felt a dose of it after 9/11, but that was in the States. The London Bombings were here, in our own country, a country many didn't believe we belonged in 'because we were Paki's', and whoever had just blown up and killed innocent people in The City had just blown up our lives along with it."

Hearing Faith share all this with me, I remembered calling friends in London to check on them and having them blame me and Abdullah for the bombings – just because we were Muslims, even though I was English and he was Arabic. Friends who we had partied with for years, friends who we cared deeply about, and who now, in the depths of fear, had chosen to associate all Muslims with the same brush, even though they were intelligent, even though they would argue that not all ravers were druggies, even though they both knew that not all men were rapists, and not all women were bitches, and not all priests were paedophiles. Their inability to distinguish between Muslims and terrorists, between their friends and terrorists, between intelligent and sane people, had shocked me, because if they couldn't – and wouldn't see the truth, then what hope did the majority of the population who didn't have Muslims as friends? The thing that became very clear to me was that even though people didn't think they were racist, Islamophobic or prejudiced, it was in times like these that the ugliness of all these characteristics raised their ugly heads and showed everyone's true colours.

"We arrived at the police station and the number of family members of those arrested from our neighbourhood surprised me. Not because they were large in number, but because there were so few of them.

'Obviously frightened that they would also be arrested,' whispered Shaista to me as we sat on the hard chairs waiting for an officer to take even the slightest interest in us being there.

After just five minutes of us sitting in the car as she composed herself, she was ready to take whatever came our way. Nothing could keep her down for long, and it was one of the many things that I admired about her. Mama may have said that she needed me, but in all honesty, it was her strength and courage that gave me the courage I needed to deal with all this. So many times people had misunderstood my quiet stoicism for confidence and a kind of certainty they themselves were looking for; and it always reminded me of how grandpa-daada would tell me, 'We are the mirrors others need for themselves my son. Always remember that because it also goes both ways. When we judge others, we are forgetting that we are all connected and that the people we are judging are playing out a potential lifestyle that could have very easily have been ours. So choose wisely. Always.'

It was his words that were cascading through my mind now. What would his advice be? I couldn't think of anything other than, 'Trust your own instincts my boy. They will never let you down. And to make sure your instinct is always as sharp as needed, make sure you eat well and healthy. They say, *trust your gut* for a reason.' And right now, my gut was churning and the coward in me was rising, but my brother Malak was in one of those cells, and he needed us all right now.

We were told we were not allowed to see him, and that he was being detained indefinitely until such time that they could prove that he was not involved in the London Bombings. And due to the anti-terror laws, they were allowed to keep him as long as they needed to – without questioning.

'But that is ridiculous!' Shaista had scoffed. 'How can you know if you have the right person if you do not question them? How can you tell your intel is correct if you do not speak with the families to be able to confirm or deny his whereabouts or his friends? This is just racism and Islamophobia, pure and simple.'

'Shaista, be quiet!' I warned her, because not only was my stomach churning it was now telling me that if she did not shut her mouth, but she would also be taken out the back and put into a cell – and that I could not allow to happen.

'Officer, I appreciate that you have intel that you have to act on, and that you would not act unfairly in this matter. We all want those lunatics who bombed our capital caught. If there is anything that we can do to help with your investigation, then please do let us know. All we want to do is help, and we know that our brother is not the person, or one of the people you are looking for. Is he active? Absolutely, if it involves climbing and things like parkour. He keeps himself physically fit by being out in nature and uses his outdoor climbing to be with nature – and to stay away from people because he doesn't like to engage in conversation about religion, politics, or even debate what to have for dinner. He is the most passive – well, other than me – in our family and his main flaw is eating too much of our mother's curry to fuel his climbing, leaving the rest of us fighting of his leftovers. I promise you; Malak is not the person you are looking for.'

The officer looked at me, and then to Shaista, as if he was weighing us up and down to see if we were credible character witnesses – or indeed suspects. 'Wait here,' he said, before heading out the back. He came back twenty minutes later and asked, 'You said your brother's name was Malak?'

'Yes, I did.'

'Okay, well, is there any other names that he is known by?'

'The only other one I can think of is *Spider* or *Guts* – the first because of his climbing and the second one because of how much he eats. My mum calls him Maluka, but he'd kill me if he knew I had told you that. Not that I mean he is capable of killing, I didn't mean that.' I quickly backtracked as I got a sharp elbow in the ribs from Shaista.

'I understand you didn't mean that,' smiled the officer and he disappeared again out the back.

When he returned thirty minutes later he asked us, 'Does your brother know much about mechanics?'

'Malak? Mechanics?' Shaista laughed out loud as if she had heard the funniest thing she had ever heard. 'Trust me officer, you do not want our brother even attempting to change a plug. He has only just figured out how to change the battery in his climbing headlamp, and I showed him how to do that!' She was still laughing as she said this. 'He didn't even know how to work the washing machine until our father showed him about six months ago. That is how good he is with mechanics. Give him a climbing harness or a bare faced rock and he will climb it in no time at all, but machines? No, Malak is not a mechanic of anyone's imagination – or nightmare!'

'Thank you for that Ma'am. I appreciate your candour. Please take a seat and I will come back to you shortly. In the meantime, there is a coffee machine over there where you can get yourselves a cup of tea or coffee from, and also a vending machine of snacks, just in case you are hungry. I do appreciate your help, and for coming down here to help us with the investigation. Just one question, do you know anyone by the name of Malik?'

My blood ran cold, and as I looked at Shaista I could tell she was feeling the same cold fear run through her as well.

'So, you do recognise that name?' The officer had spotted our recognition straightaway. 'Please, tell me who he is and we can release your brother.'

My mind ran through various different scenarios where what we were about to tell him would not make us very popular in the neighbourhood, because Malik was our next-door neighbour but one. Telling the police where he lived and who he was, and whose son he was, was not going to go down very well at all, but Malak was being held under suspicion of terrorism and there was no way he was the kind of guy to blow anything up – not even a balloon.

'Yes, I do recognise that name. Everyone in the neighbourhood will. Malik is the son of our local Imam,

Imam Haji Ahkbar. They live two doors down from us, at number 244.'

'Thank you young man. What was your name?' I gave him my name, Moana, and Shaista was stunned silent, something that would be spoken about for years to come to bring the lightness of this mood to the conversation whenever – if ever – this was spoken about.

'Do you confirm that this information your brother is correct young lady, I am assuming you are brother and sister given you said, *our brother*,' asked the officer.

'Yeah… yes, yes it is, I mean, yes I do agree. Malik is the Imam's son, Imam Haji Ahkbar,' stuttered Shaista, as white as a sheet.

'Okay, great. Well, take a seat. I won't be long.' And with that he left us where we stood, in reception, processing what had just happened, what had just been shared and what we had just done. We may have saved our brother from the police, but we had just made the lives of every single one of our family a target in the local community for grassing on the local Imam's son.

'I never did like or trust Malik,' Shaista said to me quietly as we sat back down in the seats near the vending machines, amidst the chaos of the police station.

I could already feel a glare and penetrating stare burning in my direction, and as I looked up, there was Imam Haji Ahkbar's wife and daughter, Malik's mother, and sister Nour, staring at us with the death stare, one that said they had heard everything that we had just said, and with a hatred that meant we would never be forgiven for throwing Malik under the bus with the police. We all sat there in silence, knowing that had the situation been reversed they would have done exactly the same as we had just done had it been Malik where Malak was, but it wasn't. It was Malak, and then my mind wandered. I hadn't seen Malik for the past week. My mind ran away with me, and I tried really hard not to suspect him as being one of the London Bombers, but it was hard not to. My mind started piecing bits and pieces together, but it was still really early in the morning, and I was tired, and I was not going to consider him guilty without knowing more facts about things. That just wasn't an Islamic thing to do, and it wasn't what our family did. But then again, nor was giving the police information about our neighbours and family friends which could see them detained indefinitely in jail for terrorism, and their family ostracised forever more by everyone we knew.

After about an hour, and a short burst nap by both Shaista and I, the police officer walked over to us with Malak. Shaista threw her arms around Malak crying and he squeezed her tightly, fighting back the tears and the fear. I shook the officers hand and thanked him, before turning to Malak, putting my left arm around his shoulder, saying, 'Come on man, let's go home. Mama and Babaji will be relieved to see you.'

The ride back home was a long and quiet one, each of us deep in our own thoughts and tired after the mornings events.

'I think some chai and then back to bed for everyone when we get back home, don't you?' The first words Malak had spoken since we'd left the police station.

'Yes, I think some chai and then back to bed is a great idea,' I agreed.

'Ha! You'll be lucky! Do you both really think that Mama and Babaji are going to let you go to bed after some chai without twenty questions about everything you have been asked, why you, and what's going to happen next? You are both as stupid as you look,' stated Shaista.

The statement broke the tension and made us all laugh. A much-needed laugh, and just proving that she really did know our parents better than Malak and I did.

A few more moments passed in silence, and I just had to ask the question, 'So why do you think they let you go so quickly, Malak?'

Silence.

Then, 'Honestly? Because I told them that they needed to understand the subtle differences in names between people they were arresting, rather than just thinking that a letter difference wasn't just a spelling error or immaterial.'

'You mean Malik?' asked Shaista.

'Exactly. We all know he is the one they were looking for, and just because my name looked and sounded like it, I am now going to have *arrested on suspicion of terrorism* follow me around for the rest of my life.'

The truth of that statement hung in the air and we remained silent for the rest of the journey home."

ELEVEN

ANTI-TERRORISM IS TERRORISM ITSELF

"After we arrived home and Mama had finished making a fuss of Malak, Amina busied herself over chai and breakfast, Babaji sat and watched his youngest son, noticing the shift in confidence and posture, as I had done.

Malak was different. Quieter. His playful and cocky self had gone. And it wasn't just because he was tired. It was because he had been hauled out of his bed in the middle of the night by police who had raided his family home, disturbed his parents to their wits end – especially his mother – and then bundled him into a police van in front of everyone he had grown up with, on suspicion of terrorism.

Malak was the brother who wouldn't even terrorise a spider, choosing instead to get an envelope or piece of folded paper and a jar or mug to capture it and put it back out into the garden, before wishing the spider a new adventure in the wilds. Being close to nature was one of the things he loved about climbing. He'd learnt to respect it, connect with it, and in his own words, 'Get closer to Allah, the way we are naturally meant to'.

Many times Malak and I had had conversations about our faith, and he'd often said that if people went outside more and connected with the natural world, connected with each other on an individual basis, and more importantly with themselves, then the world would be a much better place to live in.

Thinking back now, the phrase he had said to me last summer came bouldering into my consciousness like a bullet train, 'If people left religion to connect to their humanity, to their soul, then we would not have even a quarter of the problems we see in the world. The problem with Muslims, Christians, Jews and all the others that follow their holy books is that they do not know nature, they do not know themselves or what they are capable of.'

Malak and his friends had been to Snowdonia in Wales climbing, preparing for a winter climb, 'getting to know the mountain in its near nakedness' is how he'd put it. And now he had gone through this public and familial humiliation, his words burned my soul. This is exactly what he had been talking about, and now I was the one to feel the shame because his faith in Allah, in himself and in nature – all one and the same thing to him – was deeper and stronger than within me. I didn't have the depth of understanding he did, the practical implementation of the faith that he had. Nor did I have the courage he had due to his constant outdoor activities and pushing himself mentally, physically, and emotionally out on a mountain side, which had deepened his spirituality in a way none of us in the family had ever known or seen before.

The change in him was obvious to both my father and I, and Shaista. We were now seeing a member of our family in a whole new light, and a light we would never have seen had we not all been through this situation.

What he had said in the car, about the spelling of names, the ignorance of the police when it came to names from other cultures and countries, which of course extended way beyond the police forces, also applied to how people pronounced names from different cultures. Just one wrong syllable or letter could change the meaning of the name completely, and yet so very few English people had bothered to learn our names, how to say them correctly, how to spell them and what the meaning of our names were. To them, they were just names, which spoke volumes as to how little they valued names, heritage, and culture.

With the seeds of doubt planted in everyone's minds about Malak, and our family – whether these seeds would germinate and grow or whether they would die did not matter, the seeds were now planted – and just like natures seeds, it would depend upon the conditions surrounding them that would stimulate or kill off the growth. First we were tainted because of the colour of our skin, then our heritage, then the area of the country we lived, followed by the neighbourhood, the street and now the house and family name. A family name that meant honour and respect in the local area, something my father had taken pride in, perhaps too much pride, but he had built a trusted and reliable, honest and kind reputation, and now he had the opportunity to build on that. The thing was, would the surrounding neighbours be open to it, and would this bring more attention to our family in a negative way with the authorities?

No one knew what would happen moving forward and it seemed that the anti-terrorism laws which had been established in the country were now here to terrorise those of us whose skin and heritage nation were associated with the lunatics who had chosen to blow up the capital of our country, because it was our capital. This was our country, the only country I had ever known and the only country I had ever lived in. And now my family, friends and neighbours were unsafe, living in fear and ostracised by the mass media… which had already started to arrive.

Knocks on the door, the phone ringing non-stop and questions being shouted through our letter boxes and front windows. We couldn't go to the shop, out to our car and we couldn't escape even in our own home without the constant barrage of questions, microphones and cameras being pointed in our direction. We were the family of a terror suspect, except we weren't. We were the family of someone who had a similar name to a terror suspect. And that single letter in Malak's name had changed the course of our family history forever.

In the days and weeks which followed, Babaji and I found ourselves looking at each other from across the room, gave each other knowing glances, a nod here and there, and yet there was not a word spoken. Mama was still very much shaken up by the whole incident, Amina had gone into full on Mama-Watch, fussing over her like a mother-hen and Shaista was busy studying the laws which we could exploit for compensation. Malak stayed in his room, lying on his bed staring at the mountain posters above his bed.

Then one day, he came downstairs wearing his climbing gear and with his ropes and pullies bundled in a bag, went into the kitchen, and grabbed some left-over biryani and pakoras, came back in the lounge and gave Mama a kiss on her cheek as he always did when he left the house. Then he was gone. Gone back to the mountains – or peaks as he liked to correct us, 'England doesn't have mountains,' he would tell us. 'Wales has mountains, as does Scotland, but not England. We have peaks, not quite big enough to be mountains.'

In those days he would tell us that with a glint in his eye and a cheeky grin on his face, but these days, since his arrest, he was quiet, reserved, and serious.

'If we are not careful, we are going to lose him,' said Shaista as she walked into the lounge with another armful of legal books and notepads that she had been furiously trawling through and making copious amounts of notes in. 'I've been documenting how this has all affected him and I think we should sue the police.'

'Now listen, we do not want to be messing with the police any more than has been done. Your brother just needs time to process what has happened. I do not think...'

'Yes, but Babaji, what Malak is going through is something called PTSD, Post-Traumatic Stress Disorder, we all are. What they did to him, to our family is not right, and if we do not stand up to them, then these anti-terror laws are going to not only cause more trauma in families like ours, but can also lead to more and more individuals who had never given these evil terror attacks a second thought becoming the very people who commit them – because they are traumatised, because they are fed up with the fingers being pointed at them, at us, and because they are fed up with the colour of their skin being the thing that makes them a terrorist. Have you not seen the amount of anti-Pakistani, anti-Muslim and anti-immigrant slogans being spray painted everywhere? Have you not seen the looks we all get now? Have you not had more people spit on you as you walk the streets or have them cross the road to avoid you, with their eyes on you just to make sure they are watching to see if you put a piece of rubbish in the bin? Have you …'

'Now that's enough!' shouted my father, the first time I had heard him raise his voice in our home since the police came barging into our home on that fateful night in July. 'Yes, I understand. Yes, I have seen, and yes, I may be old but I am not stupid young lady. This is impacting all of us, inside this house, on our streets, across the city and the country. You would have to be blind to not see how it has impacted and divided this country. And yes, I know this is what the powers that be want…'

At this final statement, Shaista looked up having had her head lowered as father chastised her with his tone and volume of voice. She didn't realise that Babaji was as sharp as to notice that the system was pulling some very serious strings of division. Looking at her, looking at our father – as if for the very first time – tears filled her eyes and she dropped her books and notepads into the armchair beside her and threw her arms around him.

'Oh, Babaji, forgive me please. I am just trying my best to help our family in the only way I know how. I feel useless, and if I don't do something, then I am going to go crazy. I am book smart Babaji, not like you, or Faith. I am not a fusser like Amina, and I cannot stand Mama being so fragile and tearful. I have to do something and this is my offering to this whole situation.' Tears were falling from her eyes and her shoulders were shaking up and down.

I don't think I have ever seen my sister in such a state before. She was normally the strong one, the one who held me together. Had any of us ever really seen each other before? Had this home invasion ripped off the coloured lenses we had been looking at each other through all these years? Or had we simply taken each other for granted all these years? Perhaps these events had made us all own our own individual powers on an even greater scale and so they were becoming more prominent, and we were finally choosing to not take ourselves or each other for granted any longer. Whatever had happened, Malak had left the house to go climbing, the first time since the home invasion, and that was surely a good thing.

The neighbourhood had been very quiet since the raids on our homes. What had once been a real community, in and out of each other's homes, doors open with neighbours chatting on doorsteps and laughter had in the shops with one another, everyone had gone inward, either with shame because their son or daughter was still locked up in prison, or with suspicion and fear of one another – which I always thought amounted to one and the same thing.

We had become afraid of our own thoughts, our own

questions. We had been terrorised by the events of that night, by the media stalking our family members, by the looks of doubt on one another's faces and by each other. The police had broken our community and broken our spirits, and where we should have come together as a community in these difficult times, we were afraid to congregate, afraid to drop food parcels off to one another, afraid to go to the mosque, afraid to be who we truly were, and I had had enough of it. So had Shaista, and so had our father. It was time for us to do something, and the more I thought of Shaista and her legal action idea, the more I liked it. I knew Babaji would never go with it, so I thought about what grandpa-daada would do, and then I had the idea of writing to the media, or organising a press conference, of inviting the local headmasters, shop owners and police force together, to show them who we were. We had to take action, and we had to come together like we did during Ramadan, and the moment I thought of Ramadan, which was just a few weeks away, I knew what I had to do. I had to put our faith into action and show them who we really were and show them the subtleties of our language and how the outdated practices of a lot of the older Muslims were no different to the outdated practices of the older non-Muslims. I had to build those bridges of consciousness, just like grandpa-daada had taught me to do.

'What are you so deep in thought about?' Shaista had found me looking out the landing window at the top of the stairs.

'Oh, you know, the recitations we are made to do

rather than deep reflection and internalisation, the language barriers, antiquated practices in the Ummah and all the things we are hated for, but heck do we make a great biriani!'

'Oh, I love the sarcasm. But seriously. What are you thinking about?'

'Exactly what I just said. What are the things which have led to all the division between the Muslims and non-Muslims? What was it that had Malak arrested? What was it that has so many Muslims follow all the antiquated, cultural aspects of what they think is Islaam, but isn't? What is it that is needed right now more than anything, going on what you were saying about the legal case, and what Malak said in the car that shut us all up?' I answered.

It was the first time, Moana, that I had seen that look in my sister's eyes, that look between pure admiration, respect, and excitement, blended with a hint of dangerous playfulness. And it was in that moment that I knew she was going to run with exactly what I was thinking about and then take it to the very next level in a way that only she could.

And I was right.

And that is when the first of our Community Cohesion and Police Liaison events started.

And after that first event, that was when I knew that I could not stay in England and watch everything unfold the way it had been. Seeing my sister light up like that, I wanted to see that in other females. I wanted to share what I had realised with Malak, and I wanted people to know what he had said, about how when we leave the religion behind we discover our true faith. Faith in ourselves, faith in each other, faith in nature and faith in the universal connection between us all. So many are so wrapped up in their own cultural understanding of what they think is Islam but they do not even understand the language in which it is written and yet they espouse all these dogmatic… oh why am I even sharing this with you? I know I am preaching to the choir on this."

Shortly after learning about what Faith, Malak and the rest of their family had been through, and what other friends of mine had experienced either directly or indirectly following the 7/7 bombings had hit me hard. Many of the conversations I'd had following the arrests with those who wanted to engage me in conversation, pretty much began with, "I'm not racist but…" and inevitably what came out of their mouths was almost always racist. Some of it conscious racism, some of it unconscious racism, the inherited racism that came from the lack of exposure to different cultures and those who were not English, pretty much like my parents. Although, having said that, there were always choices which could be made as we became adults: whether we chose to continue to be racist, ignorant, or indeed ill-informed. We can either choose to remain in our righteousness and ego-centric views of others and the world, or we could choose to learn from others and find our similarities. It was one of the reasons Faith and I spoke more about cultural cohesion rather than cultural diversity. Always   highlighting   the   diversity   meant   always highlighting the differences between us all, rather than focusing on the things which made us the same, or the things we had in common, the aspects of life that bound us together as humans.

With comments such as "Fuck off back to your own country" a constant stream of narrative, especially every time there was an election, coming out of the mouths of those associated with the EDL: English Defence League, Britain First and the UKIP (United Kingdom Independent Party) members – it was obvious that the general public were still only tolerant of rather than accepting of the "bloody foreigners". Yet when it came to needing a taxi, or forgotten ingredients on public holidays such as Christmas Day, those very same bloody foreigners were very much wanted. The double standards and bigotry in Britain disgusted me on so many levels and made me want to leave time and time again. When I left, because it was a case of when, not if. I always doubted whether I would ever go back, and now as I sat here in Egypt remembering everything that I had witnessed and experienced as the wife and mother of Arabs, as a Muslim revert, as a business woman and human rights activist, as well as remembering what my friend Faith and his family had been through, I felt such a disconnect with both my country and with the religion I'd been enamoured by since the age of fifteen when I first discovered it in religious education class in school.

Seeing how the anti-terror laws had unfolded before I left England, and how they had spread across the West, especially in the United States, made me realise on a much deeper level that one man's terrorist was another man's freedom fighter; and it was playing out on every street, square and TV set across Egypt and the world as the Arab world rose up in what was becoming known as the Arab Spring.

"What confuses me more than anything Faith, is the *in*ability people have of being able to see the innocence of the majority of Muslims following 9/11 and 7/7, and that not all Arabs, Pakistanis and Indians are Muslims, but they have the ability of seeing through the mass hysteria whipped up by fictional characters in movies. They are able to be on the side of the resistance in movies such as *Star Wars*, *Star Trek*, *The Matrix* and *The Hunger Games*, and all the other movies that come out, but to side with the resistance in real life? With those who need it, such as the Palestinians. Well, that's a whole other story!"

"I hear you, loudly, you know I do. And we've had this conversation before Moana. No one considers the Malaysians as terrorists, and most people don't know that the Kuala Lumpa Towers have been designed to reflect the Islamic culture and heritage of Malaysia."

"Ha! I told you that!" I interjected, laughing.

"You also told me that when people speak of terrorists they only think of Pakistanis and Arabs, and yet the US are hardly ever mentioned by a Westerner as a terrorist – and given that the US have military bases in every country in the world, and have been at war for more than two hundred years of it's young history, I would say they are the biggest terrorists in the world… well, after the Zionists, anyway.

You know, sometimes, I wonder how this label of terrorist is any different to the word savage, or nigger, and whatever word they use for the Latinos. It's always the brown folk who are the ones who are demonised, never the white folk. And we wonder why there is so much division between the ethnicities. I can understand why so many of us brown folk distrust white people, and why there is so much racial hatred in the world We are pitted against one another all the time.

And I know that Malak doesn't follow a particular religion, but it is like he says, it doesn't matter whether he is Muslim, Christian, Jewish, Taoist, Buddhist or Atheist, people will always see the colour of his skin, the shape of his nose and associate his being a Pakistani with being a terrorist, and now this arrest… he has no escape. He cannot change the colour of his skin…"

"And he shouldn't be expected to or be made to feel like he should want to," I interrupted.

"No, he shouldn't, but so many of us do. So many of us want to be seen as who we are as individuals, not as a Pakistani, or a Paki, or a Muslim, or even worse, a Moslem! I mean what the fuck is a Moslem?! A fucking insult, that's what. White people are never defined by a religion, so they are free to be any faith they want, or don't want; but us Pakistanis and Arabs, we are automatically thought of as Muslims and put in a box named 'Muslims and terrorists', and we can't escape it. It is suffocating, and sometimes I wish I wasn't a Pakistani. Sometimes I wish I was white, just so I could escape the prejudice, the look of fear in people's eyes and the assumptions."

———

Remembering my friend share these feelings, say these words, hit me hard. Would my boys feel this way at some point in their lives? A white mother, different coloured brother and father? The four of us, all different shades of 'chocolate', as a young boy had innocently called us one day at the nursery where the boys went, wondering why our family was different to his all-white family.

Had I set my boys up to hate themselves just by falling in love with a man of a different ethnicity? An ethnicity which was associated with terrorism just because of the actions of a few? Was this what my black friends were going through, but instead of being terrorists, her children would grow up being suspected of being gangster drug dealers just because they were black?

Although it wasn't the same, the white privilege which presented itself as admiration, respect and adulation just because I was a white British female teacher here in Egypt, and therefore seen as better than my Egyptian colleagues, had made me uncomfortable.

None of us can escape the colour of our skin, and for some of us, the ignorance of the masses puts us in an unescapable prison that leads to self-doubt, self-hatred, and a lack of self-worth, and that had to be the worst impact terrorism has had in the world, a terrorism not created by bombs, suicide bombers or the military, but terrorism created by the mainstream media, which as Faith and I knew, was ninety-six percent owned by the Zionists. Muslims, Arabs and Pakistanis didn't stand a chance… until there was a shift in media ownership to address the bias in reporting.

Would that day come?

And if it did, when would that be?

And how many Muslims, Arabs and Pakistanis had to apologise for simply being born?

TWELVE
ALIEN:ATION

"Malak's visit to the Peaks to go climbing was becoming more and more regular, and he had started to climb higher and take on more challenging rock faces. He told me that when he climbed his concentration was so strong that he had no choice but to forget about the arrest and those few short hours of being detained by police, the abuse they had inflicted upon them all, and the beatings that some of them had received. He told me that some of the prisoners wouldn't be released for a couple of weeks even if they were cleared of suspicion because they were so badly beaten during their arrests by the police officers, that their injuries would need to heal first. With each climb, with each footstep up on the rock face, he was one more step away from the trauma. And he needed that.

I needed that. We all needed it. I envied him and how he was healing his pain through climbing, only in a small way as it felt such a great honour that he chose to open up to me Moana. It is when it is just the two of us, walking in the Peaks, and far enough away from anyone else that we cannot be overheard. They remind me of the private conversations we kids all had with our parents growing up. The way they would make time for the both of them to just be with us each on our own. The fear I would see on his face, the tears that well up in his eyes, I have never seen him like this, ever. The cheeky, playful Malak has gone, and I don't know if we will ever get him back. I hope part of him will return because I miss my cheeky – and annoying – baby brother. I know the arrest made him grow up quickly, turning him into a man, but I just hope he doesn't lose that playful, cheeky nature, for his sake, as much as anyone else's."

Hearing Faith's voice waver as he shared this with me caused my own emotions to well up and bring tears to my eyes.

"Mama went out into the city the other day, trying to get some normality back in her life, and as she went into the shopping centre, she was spat on by some yobs who told her to fuck off back to her own country, before calling her a Paki terrorist. I was so glad it was Amina who was with her and not Shaista, because Shaista wouldn't have been able to keep her mouth shut, and you know they would have both been beaten. You know, Mama now refuses to go into the city, even though Shaista keeps telling her that each day she hides, the racist yobs win. But Mama is not strong enough, and Babaji consoles her the best he can, but he doesn't know what to do for the best. We seem to have lost ourselves in the grief, and this life we are living at the moment is so alien to me. To us all. It is like my whole family has lost itself Moana, and I don't know what to do to help bring it back together. I often find myself thinking, 'If only Grandpa-daada was here. He'd know what to do.' And it is in those moments that I remember the highest truth that we are all aliens, on a fiery rock hurtling through space clinging on for dear life – without even knowing it.

These private conversations that Malak and I have been having have shown me our evolution, the multifaceted sides of ourselves, and has shown me how much we have all grown up in the past few months, the past few years in fact. It has crept up on us all so quickly, just how we are now adults, except of course Amina, who herself will be an adult in the next few years. Our family is changing rapidly and I don't know how I feel about it Moana."

"It happens to the best of us Faith, to all families, and I know that I cannot relate to what you and your family are going through, what with the home invasions and everything, nor can I relate because I was the first one in my family to leave the family home, but becoming a mother and watching Salah and Marai grow up so quickly, knowing that my baby boy Salah will be starting school in Egypt when we get there in a year's time, that's a scary thought. Before we know it, you will be getting married, having kids and watching them go through the same process. Life on repeat Dude, life on repeat."

"I don't see myself getting married or having kids Moana, and even though I want a family, I just don't see it. And that in and of itself unnerves me and makes me wonder why I cannot see my life past the next few years. Still, Ramadan is coming up soon, and we know the powerful impact fasting has on us, our manifestation process and visualisations. Speaking of which, Shaista is organising a community iftar every Thursday during Ramadan. She believes we need to come back together as a community, to heal together, and I agree with her. There is strength in numbers, and healing through the power of prayer is what we need to do to amplify the power of it. We need to bring the neighbours together, to unite them to come out of these police raids and the alienation from the rest of British society and mainstream media persecution together. We need to lean on one another as we lift each other, and by throwing herself into her new social activism and politics she is healing herself, probably without even realising it."

"Yeah, I have seen the press coverage and how the programming is vilifying Pakistani communities. It is ugly, nasty and I am disgusted that more and more people have not been able to see through the Islamophobia and racism. Is there any wonder that I have chosen to switch off from it? Honestly, being a spokesperson for the local BBC is becoming a tad tedious to be honest. The token efnik, white enough to be accepted, but efnik enough to relate. It makes my skin crawl, it really does."

"This is new territory for everyone though Moana, and none of us know how to deal with this. It is one thing to have PTSD as an individual, but as a community, one which was so close, and is now shattered is another. So magnify that PTSD across the mono-cultural white, Christian communities and we have a huge stew of fear and mistakes being made. People are being alienated, they are being bullied, ostracised, and excluded, and just like we have our trauma points, as do everyone else. Ha! Listen to me, I sound like my dad."

"Wise words spoken as usual my friend, wise words. And there are worse things in the world than sounding like your dad. He'd be very proud of you. And you know it!"

"Yeah I do. And I was reflecting on this the other day. Both Malak and I are very much like our dad. Malak has gone deep within with his climbing, his isolation, getting stoned, giving himself time to be with his thoughts. His own kind of dhikr, just like our dad. Not the getting stoned bit though, can't imagine my dad getting stoned. But Malak did get me thinking that we need to have a dhikr session Sufi style at the iftar that Shaista is organising, so I have been going through grandpa-daada's books, pulling out verses of Qur'aan, quotes from Ghazali, Runi and Lings to put up around the community centre, and for us to do the recitations together in a circle. Shaista is collating images of us all over the years as a community, some of when Mama and Babaji were first married and she's enlisted the help of some of the others in the neighbourhood. It feels good to be doing something positive, and learning about each other, the neighbours, some of their achievements, the laughter they have all shared, previous iftars, weddings, mosque and business openings. It is going to be a very special iftar Moana."

I remembered how his mood had changed so many times during that conversation. One moment he was close to tears, then fired up with the organisation of the iftar, and all the plans, the hoped-for outcomes, and the community action happening. As he was talking about the community action, I saw a side of him I hadn't seen before, and a change that I am not even sure he was aware of. It was as if his soul was calling him forward to embody something about himself that his human form had not yet caught up with. I could see the pressures disappearing and the life in him being restored. He was finding his purpose and I knew it wouldn't be long before there was going to be a big change in his life.

"The iftar went ahead and in many ways was a huge success. Most of the families had come out to break their fast together, to see each other in a beautiful and meaningful way. They had prayed together, cried together, laughed together and friendships that had been strained since the arrests, were now being restored with even more love and acceptance.

Ideas for more get-togethers to overcome all the testing times they were facing, the adults at work, the kids at school and university, and just as individuals as they went about their daily business. It was suggested that the neighbours log all the details they could remember about the harassment and attacks which were taking place. Things such as where it took place, what the attackers looked like, things that were said, and if at all possible photos and video footage being captured. The police wanted to do something about it, because not only had they acted with fear and a desire to get the bombers, forgetting professionalism, they had also destroyed some great relations that had been built over the years with the Pakistani and Muslim communities. Shik's were being attacked, so were Hindus. Community relations had been a mess ever since and it was time to rebuild, for each other and with each other.

During one of the Community Cohesion and Police Liaison Events information had been shared by the locals about the attacks and arrests had been made. Most of those arrested had belonged to the English Defence League, as well as Britain First, two of the most extreme right-wing Nazi and fascist groups in Britain. There was some media reporting but not enough. So Shaista being Shaista started blogging about what was going on, started sending her blogs to national newspapers and radio stations, and it worked. More media coverage was being given to it and she started her career in politics. Ha! My sister the politician. Mama and Babaji were so proud of her, we all were, and it was finally great to hear the comments of how she had been 'siding with the pigs' come to an end. Many times she had been accused of betrayal, of committing treason against Muslims and of being a 'coconut', but she really did show the strength that we all knew she had, but with political activism, she had a framework to channel it, to focus it and she really was making a difference.

It seemed that the more Shaista got involved with local politics, Malak would climb more, and he started having a fan club that would want to go climbing with him, so he took a few of the older boys and girls out with him. At first he was worried about being accused of 'grooming' them into the next wave of terrorists, but when the grades at school started to go up for these kids, and their focus and respect for themselves, nature, teachers and of course the adults in the community, it was obvious that Malak was a natural teacher. He still didn't pray the five times a day, nor did he go anywhere near a mosque. His place of worship was the rock face, the Peak District and his congregation were his climbing pals and the kids he taught.

He started studying for his teaching degree because he knew the kids needed a new kind of adult role model and not one of the elders, who with good intentions, just did not know how to relate to the kids in Britain. They had not been raised in Britain, so how could they relate?

Amina was still figuring out what she wanted to do, but we knew she would go into a career such as nursing or becoming a doctor, which left me wondering what I was going to do with my life. I loved community work, I wanted to inspire minds – but more than anything, I wanted to leave England. I just couldn't handle the bigotry and the racism. And I hated being called Paki, hated being expected to conform to either a devout Muslim who was always 'off to mosque' or a 'drug dealing pot head'. I wanted to disappear into the masses, become invisible, and like Malak I wanted to help kids. I just didn't know how I could do that in England. Teaching isn't my thing, but community projects are. Youth education events are, helping others understand the world around us, how insignificant we all are in the grand scheme of things, and how connected we are. I also want to learn more about the mystics, and so the only place I knew this could happen was back in Pakistan."

That's when he told me he was leaving England, and as I was heading to Egypt, there was no real point for him to stay any longer. We had become deep friends, and we knew that we both had to leave England for our own sanity, for the sake of our souls and to become the people we knew we could not become in England.

This wasn't just about leaving England for an adventure, this was about discovering and becoming who we truly were. We knew that the questions we both asked, the way we felt about religion – and our home country – was suffocating us both, and if we didn't leave, we'd kill ourselves on a deep and soulful level.

THIRTEEN
PERSONAL PILGRIMAGE

"'Are you ready Babaji? Do you have everything packed properly? Is there anything I can get you? Do you have enough underpants?'

Honestly, my mother was driving me crazy with all her questions. Why is it our parents always have a way of making us feel like a small child with their fussing, and their telling offs? I mean, she hasn't asked me about my underpants for years, and now I am heading overseas, she is asking me about my underpants!" laughed Faith.

"Oh, bless her. Your mum is just adorable, and I bet you were blushing when she asked you about your underpants!" I laughed back.

"Don't you know it! I know she is nervous bless her, but honestly, she has nothing to worry about. I will be fine."

I could tell there were nerves and apprehension in his voice. For someone who had never seen himself as a teacher, he had really thrown himself into the preparation to work with Teachers Without Borders, and submitted his lesson plans, his preferred locations in the country, and his preferred topics to teach. His preparation had been admirable. He had taken extra classes himself to brush up on his own knowledge. Had taken the Cambridge Teachers Knowledge Test, completed the Cambridge English Language for Teaching Adults, even taken lessons with an elder from the mosque to learn Punjabi and Pashtu so he could converse with people at all levels of society when he got to the more remote areas.

"This will help me integrate better and help people to trust me, well, I hope so." He'd said, and he believed it would. His parents were really proud of him, and his departure had brought them closer together.

"The only thing that is doing my head in Moana, is Babaji is more nervous than I have ever known him. He keeps pacing and saying he has a bad feeling about all this. I've never seen him like this before. He is making me nervous!"

"He just loves you; you know that. This is his way of knowing that he is letting the son he has raised go out into the big wide world by himself. It is a transition for him too, you know. You've been his pride and joy, the son he is most proud of, always… especially after what happened."

"I know. I know it is hard for him, and I know this is bringing up a lot for him as a man, a father and as a protector, but I can't live in the shadows forever, hiding from the world in my books and not going out into the big wide world. And like you say, everything happens for us. Everything. I now get to help others with what I and the others went through, otherwise it would have been for nothing. I've done a lot of healing, a lot of forgiveness, and this journey of self-discovery, this inner pilgrimage, has taught me a lot, about myself, about others and about the abusers within religion."

When he had spoken of the abusers, I had been taken aback. Had he been sexually abused in the mosque? He'd seen my reaction, and quickly corrected me.

"It's okay Moana, I wasn't sexually abused, mentally, spiritually and emotionally yes, but never sexually, unlike so many others in the hands and congregations of the various religious leaders of the world. During recitation lessons, when we were made to recite Qur'aan time and time again, never allowed to question what we were learning, or even learn the language, I and a few others were always shut down, shouted at, called infidels, and non-believers. We were bullied, mocked, shamed and tormented about our stupidity. We were told that Allah doesn't love those who question, who disrespect their elders, and this is why he hadn't given us the gift of being able to remember and recite the Qur'aan. We were being taught to hate the country of our birth because it was the land of the infidels. Being made to kneel on the floor and recite over and over again, until we had not only learnt the verse, but the whole chapter was so painful, and often we would be crying in pain, only to receive a slap around the back of the head. Or if Imam was in a really bad mood, he would press down on our shoulders so the weight on our knees created even more pain. After a while, we would numb out, and use the techniques Grandpa-daada gave me to be able to ascend."

"Ah, that's why you are so good at it," I added.

"Yep. It was one of the reasons why Malak stopped going, and why many of the girls will always wear jeans.

They have scars on their knees. Looking back now, I can see how so many of Imam Haji Ahkbar's younger congregation have become so angry, and why our community had been falling apart, had become so divided. I can also see why so many are afraid to not do as he tells them, because if this is what he did in front of others, I would hate to think what he did to those he took aside and got really angry with."

Faith paused for a moment to collect his thoughts.

"Hindsight is an incredible gift Moana – and it is just a shame it comes afterwards, rather than before, which is why I guess we are taught to keep thinking of seven excuses all the time.

One of the reasons I have learnt so much about Arabic history, culture and language is so I can truly connect with the origins of Islam, and when it is combined with everything else I have learnt about metaphysics, the quantum realm, astrology and geography, not to mention human behaviour, then I hope to be in a place of being able to help others discover the beauty and nuances of the scripture and encouraging them to find their own faith within themselves, nature and ultimately discover what faith means to them."

"The fact that you have done all this learning, and still say, 'I hope to be in a place of being able to help,' says a lot about you, Faith. Many do not have half of your knowledge and believe they are most definitely qualified to teach people about religion and faith. Just remember that. Your humility will go a long way, as will you desire to keep on learning. Your curiosity will encourage curiosity. Trust that. Have faith in that."

"Thank you, Moana. Really, thank you. I am filled with many doubts about who am I to teach these kids, but I know that not only am I book smart, I am also human smart, especially everything I have learnt from Grandpa-daada and what we went through after 7/7. I know I haven't travelled a lot, but I believe the essence of teaching is knowing more than your students and discovering and learning together. So, I am trusting that whatever questions do come up in the classroom that I am unable to answer, my students and I will be able to answer together. Ha! My students. Did you hear that? My students! I am going to be a teacher Moana, a bloody teacher!"

He sat there with a bewildered, joyful look on his face that made his baby face look even younger than ever. He looked radiant. Excited and all traces of doubt and fear were gone. My friend was ready to go and make his mark on the world.

"I know that Grandpa-daada will be really pleased with me, and that all the hours we spent in dhikr and deep in the metaphysics and mystical is because spoken language, whilst being a gift of understanding and connection, it is really a restriction. When we connect to the energy, our higher frequencies then we really truly get to be everything we were born to become. I have been studying for this my whole life, and now I get to speak about it all. It is the fuel for this fire raging within me, and all those tribal antiquated Imams have done so much harm, have abused so many of us with psyops, instilling fear into us on a daily basis, that now I am in a position of clarity, thanks to Malak, Shaista, Grandpa-daada, and the forgiveness of Mama, the silence of Babaji, and the love that we all have as a family for everyone, I am not angry anymore. I actually feel sorry for them all, that they have to abuse kids. Whether they are imams, priests, vicars, rabbi's, nuns, monks or whatever religious role they take, they are the ones with the corrupted souls, the deep layers of fear. It is why they are so zealous. They do not have the love of God, Allah, G-D, Universe or Source. They are the ones who need to find love in their hearts, practice the teachings in our holy books."

"PsyOps are dangerous, that's for sure," I replied, not quite sure how else or what else to say. He had done a lot of inner work, had been on an incredible journey, even since Amira and I had met him. Using his power to fuel his research into religious abuse, the sleazy behaviours such as the constant touching, the mind manipulation, the seduction, and the threats made, which kept all the kids under control, all of this had propelled him onwards to make a difference. And now he was ready to share everything he had learnt with those in the most remote areas of Pakistan.

I wasn't sure how that would help the rest of the world, or how he saw his vision unfolding, and when I asked him about his future vision, he said he couldn't see beyond the first couple of years. Would take each day, week and school as they happened.

And now, I wonder if the reason he could not see beyond the first couple of years, was simply because there was no future beyond the two years. His lack of vision wasn't because he couldn't see, but because he wouldn't live long enough.

During his first month in Pakistan I'd heard from him a few times, and then with my move to Egypt, keeping in touch regularly had been difficult. Getting the residential visas sorted, the boys settled into schools – and after the endless red tape and bureaucracy had been sorted out, we then started looking for our own apartment. All this as Faith was dealing with similar situations upon his arrival in Pakistan. By the time we had both been in contact with one another again, it had been weeks, then months… and now… I would never hear from him again.

I had been looking through my treasure box of keepsakes and found the emails I had printed off when I'd received them from him. I hadn't known then why I had chosen to print them off, but now, as I unfolded the pages, I knew why. I held them so tightly and close to my heart, allowing the tears to fall. This would be as close to him as I would ever get again, and the realisation of this was just too much.

Taking comfort in knowing he had put his faith into action and had been loving the opportunity to pray anywhere he liked without the fear of being kicked in the head or beaten up, allowed the tears to subside so I could read the letters.

You know I said the Peak District was the best open-air mosque you can ever find Moana? Well, that was until the mountains of Pakistan! Moana it is simply majestic. No other word for it. The mountains certainly put you in your place and make you humble. I feel so insignificant here, it is wonderful!

You'll find this quite amusing, during Ramadaan we have been 'feeding the five thousand,' one of the many Ramadaan feasts for the homeless which I have eagerly gotten involved with. The connection to Christianity and the legacy of missionary work to 'save the savages' is mildly disconcerting and had made me question the TWB (that's in house slang for us Teachers Without Borders btw, just to keep you in the know!)

I did get a few disapproving looks when I asked why it only happened during Ramadaan and not all year round, as well as a few inspired looks from a couple of others who I had connected with. That led us to organise a few 'soup kitchen' style community feeds. They didn't last long because there was such a frenzy for the food, with some fights breaking out. It was then I realised why I had received the disapproving looks and realised that they were more of a 'try it and find out' kind of looks. The independent efforts we attempted did get a bit scary at times, so we started taking the food into schools with us so the kids could eat, which as you know then allows them to learn properly. There wasn't much left over at the end of each day, as the kids ate so much, which was tinged with both happiness and sadness. Happy that they were eating — and enjoyed my cooking, and I have Mama and Babaji to thank for that, and sad because I have never seen so many hungry children Moana. And these are the kids who could afford to go to the schools I am teaching in. It makes me wonder how bad the situation is in other remote parts of the country, so I am looking at maps, train and bus routes (not to dissimilar to Egypt I imagine) and figuring out where I can be of most help to the kids and the community.

I have marker points on my journey, or as you like to call them 'anchor points' so I will make sure that I still get to visit those places so I can touch base with Mama and Babaji — who incidentally has relaxed a little more now that I have arrived, spent time with (and no doubt, left) my Chacha zad, Zair. He introduced me to my other cousins, uncles and aunties, as well as the neighbours who were very excited to welcome me into the community. I did learn very quickly why my grandpa-daada left this side of the family behind. They are so different, more of the hardcore Shi'a Muslims than the mysticism of the Sufi's which I grew to know and love through Grandpa-daada. They are not at all like I imagined and now I understand why Zair was cagey at times during out conversations. Part of me had suspected that he was more hardcore and backwards in his views when it came to women and education and a progressive view, but it wasn't until I had spent time with him in person, that I realised that my suspicions were correct. Grandpa-daada always told me to trust my intuition, and he was right. I only stayed with Zair for a couple of weeks whilst Teachers Without Borders has processed all my 'on the ground' paperwork, and I was so relieved to be out of the family home. There really was no room for quiet contemplation or privacy, and even though I had a pretty good grasp of the language, I am not sure that the translations Zair was giving to me was as accurate as it was honest, especially when it came to the things Aunty was sharing. The girls would hardly speak with me and it gave me an insight of what I am to encounter on my travels with female students and attitudes towards females. I also now understood why I was one of very few male teachers here. So far, I have only met two other male teachers Moana. I have come to believe that male teachers are becoming a dying breed the world over Moana. I know I haven't travelled much, but the conversations I have been having since I arrived with Teachers Without Borders have been opening my mind to the teaching crisis around the world. I am convinced this trip is going to be the making of me Moana.

I know things have been hard for you getting everything set up in Egypt, because they have been a nightmare for me here in Pakistan – and I have TWB doing most of my paperwork! Hopefully, with Abdullah's grasp of Arabic and knowing how things are done in Egypt, things will not be too tough for you.

I also want you to know that the boys will both be fine in the schools. Yes, I know you are worried about them, and how they will fit in and make friends, but know your boys were not born to fit in, they were born to lead. They have you as a mother and that is the best gift for them during this time of transition.

I hear there is a rumble in the concrete jungle with protests, so just be careful! I know what you are like and you are going to get involved, but whatever you end up doing, just know I cannot wait to hear about how you are kicking arse out there, opening minds, hearts and doors for opportunities. You will become loved even more deeply than you are already, so stay safe my friend, be well and continue to be your amazing self.

Oh, and get that bloody book written!

With love, your brother always.

F x

FOURTEEN

CONNECTED FROM AFAR

I must have fallen asleep from crying after reading the letter, because the next thing I knew, I could hear Salah and Marai whispering about whether to make pancakes and coffee for me.

Rolling over, I heard the paper rustle and remembered the night before. The boys jumped on the bed and said, "Morning Mama!" in chorus.

"We're wondering what to make for breakfast. Did you want pancakes, or egg on toast? We are going to make coffee too," declared Salah.

"I think eggs on toast will be wonderful, thank you." I replied still half asleep. "Where's Baaba? Is he in the office?" I asked.

"No, he isn't here and we've been up for ages!" replied Marai.

I looked around the room and noticed that he had obviously not been home, so I checked my phone and there were no new messages from him. Where was he? I lay back on my pillow and allowed my eyes to close. Why had he not messaged me to let me know he was safe or going to be late? Or not coming home at all. I was getting fed up with this, and yet couldn't let on to the boys how worried I was about the work their dad was doing. I chose to believe that he was just in a remote area of Egypt covering another angle of the uprising that was unfolding, and that as he was with the BBC he would be okay. They, at least, would contact me if there were any issues with his safety.

Salah was bouncing on his knees on the bed encouraging me to get up, and Marai was already in the kitchen getting the breakfast things out and ready to make us all breakfast. School had been closed for a few weeks now because of events in the country and so the boys and I had gotten into a routine of our own. Their cooking skills had come on leaps and bounds and so had our happiness levels, especially Marai's. He hadn't been enjoying school and so having him home, them both home, has been great for all of us. I was enjoying the homeschooling and was using a lot of the teaching resources I had received from the school I was now teaching in to develop lessons for the boys.

I wondered what Faith had thought when he read the email about me teaching. Had he received it yet? Had he had time to read it? Or was he in such a remote area that he had not even been able to access internet?

Marai could tell that I was not feeling very happy that morning, and stopped what he was doing to come and give me one of his wonderful hugs. "It's okay Mama. I'll make breakfast and you go and sit down." Before calling to

Salah, who came running into the kitchen in his underpants, asking, "What?"

"You need to set the table while I make breakfast and coffee. Mama is sad."

Salah turned to look at me, and asked "Who's died?"

That boy. His perception. His way of knowing things before even being told them. "I'll tell you everything when we've had breakfast, so whilst you both prepare breakfast and set the table, I will go and get changed out of my pj's, okay?"

"Okay!" they both said in unison, looking at each other and then again at me before getting on with the tasks at hand.

"Well, it's not Baba who's dead, that's for sure!" whispered Salah, not very quietly.

"No, you're right. Maybe it is someone back in England, or maybe it is Ms Amira?" Marai whispered back.

"Nah, it's not Ms Amira. It is someone from England. I am sure of it," replied Salah running to the dining room with the cutlery in his hands.

"Salah don't run with knives in your hands, otherwise you could be dead next." Marai called out after his brother.

Having gotten dressed, I helped take the breakfast to the table with the boys and we did our gratitude flood of saying why we were happy, started by Marai with a look towards me, with one of his air kisses. "I am happy because we get to eat breakfast together AND we all had a lie in!"

It was the first time I had checked the time, "Ha, we did, didn't we!"

"I am happy because Marai has cooked the eggs properly, and they taste great! Thank you Marai!"

"You're welcome. Mama, what are you happy for, even though you are not very happy at the moment?" asked Marai.

"I am grateful and happy because I have two wonderful boys as my sons, and we all got to wake up this morning to give life another go," I replied, doing my best to fight back the tears.

"So, who died then?" asked Salah with toast crumbs on his chin and egg in his mouth.

"Faith died. You know my friend who went to live in Pakistan to teach? He has died," I replied allowing the tears to fall.

"You mean the one with the big nose? The funny one who always played with us?" asked Salah.

I let out a little chuckle because Faith did indeed have a big nose and was always playing with the boys. "Yes, him."

"Did he get murdered?" asked Marai, "Or did he have an accident?"

I was shocked by his question, so direct, but so full of knowing. I looked at him and said, "Well, you are both smart enough to know and understand what happened, or what is *being reported to have happened*. You know he was helping people learn more about the differences between faith and religion, well, some people didn't like that, and so it is believed that he was, what they call, stoned to death."

"You mean people threw stones at him, not the kind of

stoned you and Baaba get?" asked Marai, which again made me smile and chuckle to myself.

"Yes, the newspapers are saying it was him, and that people threw stones at him." I replied.

"Well, newspapers get it wrong all the time Mama, so maybe it isn't him. Maybe the newspapers are lying again," Salah added, throwing his arms around me and giving me a big kiss, and leaving toast crumbs on my cheek.

"Sticks and stones Mama, like the nursery rhyme says, so maybe he is just broken, not dead." Added Marai.

"They are pretty sure it is him, so we just have to be thankful that we got to have him as part of our lives." I said, holding back the tears.

"Well, he was a really nice person, and he made us all happy. Remember he would say that it didn't matter if we were alive or dead, that we would all be connected, just like he was with his grandpa-daada," Marai reflected wisely.

"Yep, just like in prayers, thoughts and wishes. And when we are away from you Mama, all we have to do think of you and our hearts get happy and so that's all we have to do now," said Salah, squeezing me that little bit tighter, whilst getting comfy on my knee.

"Salah, you are getting too big to sit on Mama's knee."

"No, I am not!"

"Yes, you are!"

"No, I. AM. NOT."

"Yes, you are!"

"Not."

"Are."

"Not."

"String."

"Necklace."

"Mama!"

"Family!"

And so the word association game had begun, and my heart filled with gratitude because this had been one of the games we played to stop the bickering amongst them. A game which Faith had seen unfold before him in one of our car journey's which had led onto a really random game of "I spy with my little eye", a game he had said was so British.

As the word association game continued, and breakfast came to an end, I realised that Salah had nailed it when he said that we were all connected through wishes, thoughts and prayers. I knew that I could meditate to reach a higher consciousness, and through that I could find peace, and that I could receive spiritual messages from him by being connected to the higher consciousness. It is what we had spoken about so many times, and yet now, this would be the only channel we would have moving forward.

If I could create a new reality by harnessing the power of energy, through manifestation, then I could connect with my friend through meditation… if I ever got to that level of the ascension process.

I knew we were all connected, all one, and when we got out of our heads and truly, deeply into our heart spaces we could achieve anything. I knew that with the amount of things going on around me at the moment with the Arab Spring unfolding, and the uprising here in Egypt, I would not be able to focus properly. There was too much going on, and without Abdullah here to help take some of the pressures off, or to talk to about what was happening, it meant I had to deal with a lot by myself.

Being reminded by my boys that I was still connected to Faith through prayers made me even more grateful for my boys, who were now clearing the table ready for a game of Monopoly. The love and understanding they had about so many things, made me grateful that I was parenting them the way I chose to. I enjoyed our open and honest conversations, and I enjoyed watching them process information. They were teaching me a lot and showing me new ways of dealing with things.

They gave me hope, and most of all, they gave me faith in the future.

I didn't know what my faith was going to morph into with all the questions that had come up for me since arriving in Egypt and meeting Maha, a new Sufi friend, but I knew Faith would have loved her.

I looked at the clock, and saw it was now coming up to lunchtime, and we had only just finished breakfast. Abdullah still wasn't home, and I still hadn't heard from him. And to be honest, the way I was feeling, I had gotten past wanting to share this grief with him. He didn't know Faith, and so what could he say?

The only thing I did know was that whatever happened moving forward, I had to have faith in myself, in the Universe and in my boys, because without faith, what else is there?

GRATITUDE

The deepest gratitude I have will always go to my two son's Khaalid and Naasir for the endless encouragement, love, motivation, and inspiration they gift to me daily.

Combined with the belief they have in me, with the words 'You always come up smelling of roses' from my mother repeating themselves in my mind when things get tough, I am able to remember harder times in the past where I have pushed through to achieve my end goals. Often alone.

In the moments when I look at the world and wonder why so many espouse greatness, kindness and understanding, and wonder why the world is in the situation it is in, I pray deeply for humanity and for peace.

I send deep thanks and gratitude to you, my readers for buying my books, for continually seeking answers and for choosing to open yourselves up to the truth behind the smiles. Some of us are blessed to be able to afford therapies, counselling and education, and some of us learn how to heal and about the world through books. Your continued purchases of my books, reviews and messages help me going on this journey, because often as an author this life feels pointless. Thank you for keeping me motivated to deliver more content for you and to others, so I can keep going to make a difference in the world.

As always, I am grateful to Jerry Lampson for his amazing design talents, and Linda Diggle for being my right-hand woman in keeping me sane, organised and learning through the publishing process.

And one final thank you to Jeff, Mike, MacKenzie and Jen, and fellow crew members of Via Rail Canada for their kindness, conversations to keep me sane and keeping me in endless cups of tea as I wrote the final parts of this book crossing Canada from Halifax to Vancouver, and from Vancouver back to Winnipeg to head north to Churchill on the following trains: The Ocean, The Canadian and The Hudson Bay. You will be remembered always.

ABOUT DAWN BATES

 Dawn Bates is an award winning, international bestselling author and publisher of more books than she can keep count of, on five continents.

She specialises in developing authorities who wish to give a voice to the voiceless, working with them to create brand expansion strategies through activism, authorship, and business.

With a cheeky sense of humour, a love of deep ocean sailing, Dawn dances though life whilst specialising in social justice and human rights, which underpin everything she does. Her study with the University of Oxford, where she's working towards her PhD, combined with her impressive world travels, ensures her books are powerful.

Dawn brings together the multi-faceted aspects of the world we live in, delivering mic dropping inspiration, motivation, and awakening. Her work captures life around the world in all its rawness.

To discover more about Dawn, please visit: www. dawnbates.com. To connect with Dawn, please use: linkedin.com/in/dawnbates.

ABOUT THE PUBLISHER

Dawn Publishing specialises in books which have human rights, social change, and cultural diversity at the core. Memoirs, autobiographies, or those which are biographical in nature are welcome, as are ethnographies, historical fiction and a select few genres which empower others to own their voice and speak their truth.

We support solo and co-authors willing to invest their resources into creating excellent books which highlight important issues around the world. We do not write or publish books of a ghost-writing nature.

An international team of experts are on hand to help you self-publish with a full range of publishing services to suit your vision. Our books are not always easy to read due to their nature, but the stories need telling so we can create the positive change needed in the world.

Founded by international bestselling author of more books than she can keep count of, on five continents, Dawn Bates, you will find her brilliance for story development, exceptional leadership, and entrepreneurial skills in the DBI Author Academy – a great resource for all those looking for confidence and courage to self-publish.

Manuscript assessments are also available for those who are looking for an expert eye to help develop the book and prepare the author for the reality of being a published author.

To discover more about Dawn Publishing and our services, please visit www.dawnbates.com/writers.

www.ingramcontent.com/pod-product-compliance
Lightning Source LLC
Chambersburg PA
CBHW061447210726
48287CB00007B/2402